SUBCUTANEAN

SUBCUTANEAN
30287

by Aaron A. Reed

Printed by Amazon Kindle Direct Publishing

Typeset in LaTeX using the *novel* class by Robert Allgeyer, the NovelDeco and Mont fonts, and custom code. Cover design by the author.

First Edition(s), 2020
Seed 30287, ISBN: 9798605947820
Independently Published

Subcutanean is a permutational novel: the text can be rendered in millions of different ways. This is the version generated from seed #30287. Look in the back of the book for instructions to unlock a second wholly unique version, which might have different words, sentences, or even entire sequences.

Seed Number Key:
Seeds starting with 0: Advance Reader Copies
Seeds starting with 1: Limited Crowdfunder Editions
Seeds starting with 2: USB Key Editions
Seeds starting with 3: First Editions (Feb 2020)

The book you're holding is just one version of this story. SUBCUTANEAN is a permutational novel: there are millions of ways it can be told. This is the version generated from seed 30287.

If you're curious, you can find out in the back of the book how to get your own unique copy which might include words, sentences, even entire scenes that don't appear in this version, or play out in different ways.

But there's no need to worry about all that right now. All the books contain the same story, more or less. For now, this is the one you have.

This is the one that's happening to you.

PART ONE

DOWNSTAIRS

Icarus should have waited for nightfall,
the moon would have never let him go.

Nina Mouawad

I don't want to tell you this. I don't want to gut you, reach inside and pull things out, not again. Old wounds and sleeping dogs, you know. Tales better left untold. And you've already heard this one, even if our stories were never quite the same.

But that's what writing this is for. If it's only a story, maybe we can understand, come to terms. Make peace.

Pretend it's not ours.

I used to have these dreams, when I was young. Did I ever tell you this? I'd be wandering an endless beach of smooth white sand, unbroken but for a handful of deep and conical pits. I'd peer into these when I neared one, anxious, feet clenching the loose sand of its lip. Sometimes there'd be a puddle of murky water at the bottom. Sometimes a dark opening. Sometimes teeth. Even the ones without teeth ached with some invisible wrongness, were more than negative spaces in sand. They had energy, a primal liveness. They were hungry. I was fascinated and repelled by them, drawn to their edges again and again, toes curling, though I'd try to stay away. But they multiplied as I wandered, puncturing the flat sand more and more until they reduced it to a maze of pathways, then one of ridges. Inevitably I'd take a wrong step and start to slide, tumbling with the treacherous sand down toward the dark of the bottom, a point just large enough to slip through, to swallow me up. Almost always I'd wake before I reached it, but once I slid past pit-teeth and they bit me, sliced into my back, and I woke with a shock of pain so intense I screamed. I'd tumbled out of my bunk bed and fallen onto a half-assembled model; plastic struts had pierced my skin. I got rushed to the hospital in the middle of the night, mom in her dressing gown and me in bloody pajamas, and got ten stitches. I'd woken up too late. The pit had won.

Maybe premonition, the dreams, but I think something simpler. Even that young I'd found the fears I'd struggle with well into adulthood. Losing control. Facing the unknown. And knowing that just because something isn't real doesn't mean it can't hurt you. At four years old I told myself a story of teeth and sand traps. It would take the rest of my life to understand why.

But this story. Our story. Maybe it's a language we can speak. Find in the telling the truths that matter. Embellish, excise. Revise. Revision.

Although our story actually happened. I trust you still remember that.

Fine. Okay. You ready?

This is what happened, Niko, when we found some stairs underneath my bed, and decided to go see where they led.

Right from the start things were wrong, but I couldn't see it. Maybe I didn't want to. Or maybe I'm being too hard on myself. There wasn't exactly a roadmap for what happened to us, a script to follow. But it's undeniable that even on that very first night—the night of the Russian dance club, remember?—everything was already wrong.

I hadn't wanted to go to the club. But Niko insisted. "Russian techno, man, one night only. That new place over by the old stadium. Lots of sexy people will be there, including us." I ran out the usual litany of excuses: I had work in the morning, I had Bio homework to do, I hated going out to clubs with a burning passion. He batted them all away without any obvious effort, and so that's how I found myself pressed up against a wall listening to music so loud it hurt, arms crossed, feeling miserable, wishing I was back home listening to a Dvořák symphony instead.

When I could see him through the crowd, I watched Niko surf it, laughing, gesticulating wildly as he somehow held conversations despite the deafening racket, and dancing his ass off, mostly with girls, and once or twice with guys, whether out of politeness or genuine interest I couldn't tell. I'd never really been able to tell. He flirted with everyone, flashed the same manic energy in all directions. I'd worn my rainbow pride bracelet at his insistence, the one I'd bought a few months back and mostly been too chickenshit to wear (it was a college town but a conservative state). I might as well have worn a bag over my head, despite Niko's assurances that The Gays were almost definitely very into Russian techno, he was pretty sure. "Or maybe all those pulsing Slavic rhythms will make some drunk straight guy want to get all experimental and shit," he said, waggling his eyebrows. "Never know."

I knew. And I was right: nothing happened. No one talked to me, or even noticed me, and standing there, I couldn't imagine why they would, why anyone would want to talk to an acne-faced geek in clothes that didn't fit, leaning against a grimy wall and wishing he were anywhere else.

From across the club, Niko caught my eye, and gradually danced his way up to me, strobe lights washing out his tawny skin, twisting through his dark curls. He arrived within the eighteen-inch earshot zone and shouted something.

"What?"

He put his lips up to my ear, shouted again. "Having fun, Ryan?" He pulled back with a cheeky grin, and cackled in delight when he saw my expression, grabbing my arm. "Come on, man," he yelled, "let's get some air."

Dragging me through the crush of people, still dancing, bopping his head to the music, waving at some people and smirking seductively at others, he somehow managed to maneuver us through an impossible blockade of bodies without stepping on any toes or getting stepped on in return, toward a back exit I hadn't even realized existed, all while making eye contact every few steps to make sure I was okay. I'd never figured out how he managed to do so many things at once. Sometimes even one thing at a time was too much for me.

We pushed through a metal door into a blessed pillow of colder, quieter air, where a handful of smokers stood around chatting. I took a deep breath, more relieved than I'd expected to be. Niko pulled a single cigarette from behind his ear—he'd quit; someone inside must have given it to him—and bummed a light from one of the smokers. We walked a few paces farther out into the parking lot, enjoying the night air.

"So what's wrong?" he finally asked.

I sighed. "This isn't really my scene."

"Leaving the house isn't really your scene, yeah, I get it." He blew smoke from the side of his mouth, raising one wry eyebrow. "But you have to take chances, man. Get out of your comfort zone. I mean what was the point of coming out if you never actually *go out*?"

"Well it's fucking easier for you," I said, feeling miserable. "You can sit next to some girl in class, bump into her on the street. Say sorry for spilling her coffee, waggle your eyebrows, and boom, long term relationship."

"Yeah, that's definitely how that works," he said. "So if it's that easy, Ry, how come I've been single for the last forever?"

"Your terrible fashion sense, probably," I said, looking down at my sneakers, although truth be told it was a mystery to me too. It had been almost a year since his last relationship. Still more recent than mine. "Okay, lame excuse. I'm just... bad at meeting people. And I don't get how you're supposed to do it when the music's so loud you can't even think."

He shrugged. "Serendipity is everywhere. So give it an excuse to happen to you. Get out there, take chances. I mean there's gay people everywhere, dude, even in this shithole state. You just have to man it up and figure out who they are."

I looked up at him, startled, but he was looking away towards the horizon, expression distant, thinking about something. I looked back down at the ground before he could see me looking. *Stupid.*

"Should I take you home?" he asked at last.

"You don't need to babysit me." My mood was blackening. "I can look after myself."

"So do. No point making yourself miserable if you're not having fun."

"I thought..." I didn't know how to finish. I thought he'd wanted me to come. I thought if he were here, maybe I'd enjoy it. I thought I could pretend to be a person who enjoyed clubs, crowds, Russian techno. I'd thought, despite all evidence, that tonight would be different.

"You're right. Guess I should jet." Hoping my voice wouldn't betray what was welling up inside me, I looked up, met his eyes with the best fake smile I could muster. "Catch you later, man."

He looked straight back at me and I could tell he wasn't buying any of it.

Flicking the cigarette onto the asphalt, he ground it out with his heel, clapped my shoulder. "I'll come with you."

"No, you don't have to," I said, flooded by an awkward admixture of guilt and relief. "I'm fine. You go back in there and have some fun. Find some hot pixie chick with feathers weaved into her hair and go wild."

He shot me an annoyed look, brushing black curls back from his eyes. "Orion. I said I'm coming with you." He put an arm around my shoulder and guided me into the parking lot. "The hot chicks in there obviously have terrible taste in music, if that's what you could call what they were playing. I expect you might have some opinions about that."

"Well," I said, emphatic, and laughed, surprised at myself. At him. He had a way of turning things around like that. Defeat into victory. No into yes. Everything was better again, at least for now.

Talking, laughing, we struck out into the night for the long walk home.

We'd been friends since freshman year of college and best friends since the year after that, and by now felt like something more, placidly absorbing jokes about being joined at the hip, going everywhere together. We were; we did. Especially since his accident, we'd had a profound if unspoken level of companionship

I'd never felt with anyone. Usually I was content with that.

In some ways we had so little in common it was astonishing we'd become friends, and that led to frequent arguments, sometimes rising to breakup levels of drama. At other moments it seemed like the universe had meant us to find each other. Over the years we'd grown together, like two plants in the same small pot. It had been an especially tumultuous gauntlet of an undergrad—although I guess it feels that way for everyone—so shared roots twined us together now, half-remembered fragments of stories and selves: skipping a funeral to camp together in the rocky canyons of Brushwillow, sharing long silences amidst the lakes and pines; pulling all-nighters on mad projects with desperate stakes; driving to the next town over through a summer midnight, windows rolled down and air thrumming through, desperate to find fresh vegetables for reasons that seemed incredibly important at the time, buzzed from both caffeine and alcohol as in so many stories involving Niko. In our defense the alcohol was supposed to go in the ragu.

Walking back home from the club through the chill night air with him was a relief, and not only because the shots were starting to hit me and walking a straight line on my own would have been rough. The night felt endless, anonymous, an escape from daytime problems. In the fall we'd be starting our fifth year of college, neither of us particularly close to graduating with any particular degree, and for the first time that felt ominous. The future staked out before us our whole lives was running out. A blank canvas ought to have been exciting, but any direction we could imagine to go in seemed blocked off, already closed, inaccessible or unrealistic. Friends were picking already between the remaining well-flagged routes: getting careers, getting married, getting pregnant, getting gone to new cities, new lives, new starts. It would be our turn soon enough.

By the time we hit the top of the hill and saw the house, we were ready to be back indoors. We'd moved in a few weeks back, Niko and I and our friends, mostly his, students and lapsed students and a few brave graduates, still settling into the rambling old off-campus house we'd found in the newspaper. (Cast your mind back to a time when kids like us had figured out the internet but people old enough to own property hadn't, so instead of browsing classifieds our bandwidth went entirely to downloading all the music in the world.) I'd gotten ranty about real music on the walk back, and as we stepped through the juddering screen door, its metal-on-wood screech already a familiar sound, I had a half-dozen songs queued up to play for him.

Mentally, I mean: digital music players hadn't caught on yet back then, although it was still tragically too late for my records to be anything but anachronism. Vinyl wouldn't start making a comeback for years and was deader than dead. Maybe that was why I liked it. When we moved in I'd stacked my crates of LPs in the closet, so now as we tromped up the stairs to my room and dragged them out to hunt for the albums I wanted to play, we got drunkenly annoyed at the lack of anywhere to put them. So that was how I ended up on my hands and knees, searching for a way to open up my bed.

"Bed" was generous: it was a mattress, thrown on a raised wooden platform built into a corner of the room. Mattress-sized, it had seemed like the sensible spot to put one, but the bulky thing also really seemed like it ought to be hollow and have some storage space inside. I'd never found any handles or hinges, but in our drink-addled haze it seemed ridiculous that the thing couldn't be opened somehow, and because I can't leave well enough alone and because unsolved challenges annoy me, and, okay, because booze, there I was on hands and knees fiddling with the paneled edges of the platform, shoving and kneading and banging on them. When something finally gave with a satisfying *chunk*, I whooped in satisfaction; but leapt back startled when the whole platform groaned and swung up, pencils and organic chemistry textbooks sliding off the mattress onto the pitted hardwood floor.

Underneath was a set of steep stairs down.

"Whoah," Niko said, "Jackpot."

They were carpeted in the same dark beige as the rest of the house, which looked like someone had redecorated in the seventies and died decades later unaware style had moved on. Eleven steps led down to a landing where they twisted right and reversed. Cramped, but bland and familiar: the walls paneled in that same fake wood as the rest of the house, lit by those same tacky wall sconces. All as you'd expect from the stairs down to a basement, except we were on the second story and the house already had a basement, which emphatically did not connect through my bed.

Niko laughed in astonishment. "What the fuck is this, man? What's down there?"

"Hell if I know. More secrets." We were grinning, because this sort of thing had already happened a few times since we'd moved in. The house had been my find. The group of us were getting older (or so we thought then) and were looking to move up in the world, so we pooled our resources to go in on a house in the pleasant tree-lined neighborhood a few blocks farther out. It was an old house, maybe as much as a hundred years old, but big, in good repair, and, most important, cheap: we were all paying less rent than when living in pairs or alone. I'd claimed the funky second-floor patio room in a lumpy wing extending into the backyard, clearly a later addition, and Niko snagged a creaking and stuffy room next to mine which he dubbed "lovingly misshapen." A lot of the place was like that: a half-landing here, an awkward angle there, bits taken out and bricked over on some whim or other. The house had expanded and contracted over the generations, it seemed, in decades-long breaths.

The listing hadn't mentioned a secret passage. But it also hadn't mentioned the closet with a door in the back leading to a dusty, forgotten room (which now housed a dusty, forgotten game of Axis and Allies); nor had it mentioned the extra bedroom in the basement tucked away around a corner and behind an unlikely-looking door. These small discoveries gave the place a quirky, rambling feel, and I loved it. My whole life I'd had dreams about finding new rooms in houses I'd lived in, each time with a thrill of discovery, of learning your cozy domain still had surprises, things left to find. Maybe it came from moving around all the time as a kid. Or maybe it said something about me.

I still had them, the dreams. I didn't know they were about to get much worse.

Niko touched the angled bottom of the bed platform and looked at me, as if for permission. He gestured grandly downwards. "Well, Orion, should we check it out?"

I gave him a formal bow, the room only spinning a little. "Indeed, Nikolaos, let's fucking do it."

He grinned and tousled my hair, bounding over the lip. He stooped as he took the first few steps, black curls brushing the underside of the tilted platform.

"You going to fit down there?" I smirked. "This looks made for normal-sized people, not basketball players."

"High school power-forward Nick appreciates your validation of his identity, thanks," he called back, almost to the landing. "College dilettante Niko, though, wants to know if you're fucking coming."

I hesitated on the threshold, strangely reluctant.

He turned from the landing to look back up, arms folded. "I'm not *that* tall, am I? I've only got like three inches on you and your—" He flailed a hand up and down at me. "Your demographically average carcass. Stop giving me complexes."

Actually you're exactly four and a half inches taller than me. But who's counting.

He shrugged, continued down the next set of stairs and out of sight. "Later, skater."

I flipped his skinny ass off and followed him down.

Despite his complaints, Niko was in fact wearing a basketball jersey, but an ironic one from the thrift store, for some hopefully-fictional team called the Reagans. He wore a purple blazer over it, which I trust is all I need say about his fashion sense. Somehow, it worked. His horrifying ensembles always worked, whereas the clothes I'd buy, new or used, turned ugly, permanently wrinkled, and the wrong size by the time I got them home. "Dear LiveJournal," I'd written once in my private, locked LiveJournal account, "I get now that I'm destined to die alone. You can stop sending me signs." I had never shared my LiveJournal account with anyone and never would, which some people had told me was missing the point. Nowadays on social media I do a lot of typing and erasing status messages without posting them. Maybe you can relate.

Anyway. Niko had shrugged his shoes off when we'd gotten to my room, and now his bare feet sunk half an inch into carpet as he tromped down the stairs. His feet were hard not to notice: maybe it was all the basketball, or the Greek ancestry, but they were like statuary. Perfect.

The stairs were steep but otherwise unextraordinary. Around the corner, more of them dropped to a second landing. We stomped down, Niko's drunken excitement leading us on. Past that corner was one more landing and one final run of steps that opened into a large, windowless room.

It was bigger than any other room in the house, maybe thirty feet across by sixty or seventy long. (Logically it ought to have been the same size as the house's footprint, but both the dimensions and orientation were wrong for that.) It had the same beige carpet and brown wall-paneling, tacky faux-bronze wall-sconces, and a plaster ceiling eight feet up. Firewood was stacked up by two fireplaces on opposite walls, in the same style as the non-functional one upstairs hidden by our TV. No windows, not even those awful basement ones that fill up with dead leaves and spider webs. A smattering of old couches and end tables lined the walls, along with the expected bits of floor lint, carpet stains, wall gouges, and other subtle remnants of long occupation. A cool, musty smell suggested said occupation had been a long time ago.

Five open doorways led out: two along each long edge, and one on the far wall opposite the stairs.

"Holy shit, Ry, this is fucking amazing!" Niko's eyes lit up as he walked a few paces in. He flexed his bare toes on the ugly carpet. "It's like a whole secret underground lair!"

I felt the same thrill, tempered with hesitation. Did our landlord somehow not know about all this extra space? Was it some kind of forgotten bomb shelter? Niko was already talking about throwing parties down here, cleaning up the couches. A secret basement hangout spot.

We called it Downstairs, big D, without really thinking about it.

The architecture was making my head spin, though. (Okay: also the beer.) But someone else's bedroom was under mine. I felt an indignant vertigo, and made Niko come resolve this mystery before exploring any farther. We went back up to my room, then downstairs—regular lower-case downstairs—to reconnoiter. There was, in fact, an odd protrusion into the kitchen underneath and to one side of my room, and when we peeked into our absent housemate's bedroom around the corner, a mirroring blocky bulge in there. So together those two bulges explained the stairs, though not why you'd build a staircase in the middle of a wall like that. But the house was full of those weird angles and edges, so it seemed in character.

We went back Downstairs and poked around a few of the side hallways. Pretty cramped, but no worse than other god-awful basement apartments I'd seen students living in. Like some of those, there were no windows anywhere, which made sense: it felt too far down. Rooms opened off the sides of the halls (those cheap particle-board doors, those rattling brass-plated tin doorknobs). Some were carpeted and looked like they could be bedrooms; others had bare concrete flooring like a laundry or utility room. Most had a piece or two of abandoned furniture, all decades out of date, dusty, and anonymous.

The hallways branched at the end: we picked one and saw both ways passed more doors before making L-turns, each in opposite directions. Those crappy wall sconces were everywhere, so despite the lack of windows, it was almost too bright. They were all lit, and weirdly enough we couldn't find a light switch anywhere.

"You don't think we're, uh, paying for all this electricity?" Niko asked, alarmed.

"We haven't gotten our first bill yet." I felt proud for not slurring my speech; witty. "Good thing we're splitting eight ways."

We didn't exhaustively explore, beyond checking another hallway and seeing that it, too, branched and snaked off, shedding rooms left and right. Niko had started down that one, but I stopped, a wave of nausea washing over me, and put a hand against the cold wall.

He stopped instantly. "You okay?"

I smiled, embarrassed. "I think, uh. Don't want to get too far from a bathroom."

He eyed me appraisingly. "You shouldn't have done that last shot. I keep telling you. Beer before liquor, never sicker." He tousled my hair again, but gently. "Okay, man. Hang on just one sec. I need to see the end of this fucking hallway and then we'll get you back upstairs."

I didn't want him to leave but couldn't think of any sane reason to stop him that didn't sound needy, so I nodded and let him go. Too many vaguely ill feelings were churning around inside me to sort them out from each other.

"I'll wait here," was all I could say, the thought of walking back up twisting stairs feeling for a queasy moment like a bad idea.

He was already halfway down the hall, but lifted a hand in acknowledgment. Moments later he'd turned the corner and was gone.

It was suddenly very quiet.

I sunk to a sitting position, knees at my chin, back against the fake wood-paneling. *Why do you always, always drink too much? Idiot.* I tried to focus on the feel of the carpet under my butt, the smoothness of the wall at my back. I tried not to think about my stomach.

Please, please hurry back.

Something changed around me, subtle but significant. Head swimming, I couldn't lock on to what, at first, was different. I blinked, squinted.

The light. The play of light around me had changed, gone darker, even though none of the wall sconces in my field of vision had gone out or gotten dimmer.

We were at a T-junction, where the hall we'd come from, back to the big room with the five doorways, had branched in two directions. I was slumped against the wall facing the way we'd come, head turned towards the right-hand fork, the way Niko had gone.

I decided the dimming must have come from the lights in the hall behind me, the one we hadn't explored yet. They must have gone out.

Careful, still fighting nausea, I turned my head.

I've always had an unhealthy imagination. This has manifested itself in various ways over the course of my life. Staying under the covers reading comics instead of doing homework, or sleeping. Satisfying myself with vivid fantasies about guys I crushed on rather than risk asking them out in real life. Obsessions, where each new hobby would become all I could think about. Things get lodged in my head and they stay there, sometimes for too long.

The unexplored hall was dark. The lights were off, and the

dark brown walls sucked up the refracted light from the other two hallways, so that the end of this one, where it turned another corner, was right at the edge of shadow.

But there was enough light to see that someone was standing there. Back toward me, facing away.

I stared and tried to unsee the human shape, to resolve it into a trick of angles and darkness: turn off my brain's over-eager pattern matchers, finding predators in a coincidence of edges. It didn't help that the hallway was spinning and I felt closer and closer to throwing up each second.

It moved.

The shadow took a step backward, coming closer. Careful. Hesitant. I couldn't see its face because it was turned away. But I realized anyway who it was.

Maybe my eyes had adjusted to the dim light, or maybe my imagination was shifting into a higher gear. But like the solution to a puzzle plunking full-formed into my head I recognized, now, who was standing there at the end of the hall.

It was me.

I clutched the carpet under my hand, feeling for the solidness of it, an anchor back to reality. Everything was spinning. My stomach churned and my mouth filled with saliva, like the glands for adrenalin and poison protection were crossing wires. Fight, flight, or puke.

The face was still hidden but I recognized the way the body held itself, the silhouette it made, the shoes. Unmistakable. The person in the mirror, except I'd never seen him from this far away before, or from this angle.

I squinted into the darkness, seeing something else now. Something barely visible, even deeper in the shadows.

There was more than one of them.

The second stood just behind the first, so I couldn't see its face either: but it was the same silhouette, the same height, the same shape. It was another one, identical. Another me. It had been there all along, hidden behind the first, and I could only see it now because they were moving again, lifting up the other foot, still slow, still hesitant, following the double in almost perfect synchronicity. Like they were glued together.

They put the feet down, gentle, soundless on the thick carpet. Another pace closer. Still turned away.

Seeing double. You're drunk. Except I'd never had it happen in three dimensions before, along the z-plane. And the edges of the hall weren't doubled at all.

I wondered how many more were stacked up behind them. How many more I couldn't see, each pressed up against the last, a line vanishing into the darkness, stretching back god knows how far, patient, waiting for something I could never understand.

I wondered what they wanted.

I wondered how fast they could reach me if they started to walk backwards, toward me, at a steady pace.

"What you looking at?" Niko asked from behind me, and I *leapt*, fucking leapt to my feet like the floor was electric, whirling around to face him, body in full panic as all the building adrenalin flooded through me in an instant; panting and overwhelmed with terror and nausea and a terrible, stabbing relief at seeing him, seeing a him I could believe in instead of a me I couldn't.

"The lights went out," I said, gasping, not looking behind me. Also, more certain: "I need to throw up."

He clapped my shoulder, grim. "Let's get you back upstairs."

I let him shepherd me away. I didn't look back down the hall.

But as we left, his arm protective on my shoulders, he frowned. "Pretty sure those lights were out when we first came down here, man."

≋ 2 ≋

Turned out Niko hadn't found the end of the hallway. It had twisted a couple more times, he said, then split again. But that was all academic while I was puking my guts out over a toilet bowl, and for much of the awful day after. Still, it might seem odd that we didn't go back down there to map the whole thing out right away. I can't really explain it, unless Niko was already feeling the same irrational foreboding as me.

Anyway. I knew there wasn't really anything down there, Downstairs, and as the hangover faded so did the lingering terror. Replacing it was a giddy sensation like having too much Halloween candy. There was a whole huge secret basement under our house that only we knew about. It felt good to have a secret. Another code in our personal dictionary, something only for us.

Niko was terrible at keeping secrets. By next afternoon, all the other housemates had seen Downstairs too, as well as a couple of his lacrosse buddies and one or two of his closest philosophy buddies. (He'd made a point of changing majors and hobbies once a quarter for the past year, while continuing to swear up and down to his immigrant parents he was still majoring in Economics.) I tried not to take the betrayal personally, but kind of failed.

But the strange thing was that no one seemed much interested. Everyone agreed Downstairs was a cool find, and made for a nice hangout spot, but no one cared to venture too far outside the big central room, or spend too much time down there. Everyone other than Niko and I would get bored, start talking about other things, eventually drift back upstairs to whatever they'd been doing before.

Odd, in hindsight.

We did end up dusting off a couple of the old couches down there, and moving down a half-dozen boxes of my records, and made the Big Room available as a kind of secondary hangout space, quieter than the crowded front room with the TV and people always coming and going. Some of the empty rooms off the big one turned into overflow storage for everyone's miscellaneous shit, but remained otherwise unoccupied. An old bandmate of Niko's who'd dropped out of college to start an art collective got really excited about free studio space, moved in a bunch of junk for some unfinished sculptural masterpiece ("I'm going to need at least twice this many fishbowls," she apologized), then never came back again. Maybe it was a con.

I didn't get on well with most of Niko's friends. I'm sure they all wondered what he saw in me.

No one did end up moving down there. Zero natural light is kind of a downer, even for well-adjusted people. Niko made some noise about bringing a girl down sometime. ("Dude, it's a secret make-out lair. You're doing college wrong if you don't get some action down there.") But we both knew he wouldn't actually do it. It was too quiet, for one thing.

It also felt forbidden, somehow, but not in like a sexy rule-breaking kind of way. Being down there had the vague flavor of trespassing, the kind where you're not going to get away with it and it'll go bad for you when you get caught. Sneaking into a restricted area at the airport; busting into Area 51. I mean it was our house, right? But Downstairs didn't feel like ours. Enough laughter or booze or noise and the feeling went away, or at least buried itself somewhere deep, where you'd hardly ever notice it.

Maybe because of that, definitely because I had to fill in

at my job for two work-studies who faked being sick, maybe also because we enjoyed prolonging the sense of mystery, and, okay, because I was sulking, more than a week passed before we got around to scoping out the place in depth. Niko spent a day in an extraordinary funk of fierce depression followed by an equally intense reversal, like he'd do from time to time, and I took advantage of his high to prod him into going to catalog Downstairs. He took to this plan eagerly, and seemed pleased when I told him I'd been waiting so we could do it together. "Ryan," he said fondly, "in an emergency, you know, you can do things without me. I'll allow it."

"Well, I kind of thought this was like, our thing, you know."

He fell onto one knee. "Oh, my noble Orion," he intoned, "canst thou e'er forgive such rank betrayal, breaking this our vow of secrecy? Will thy gentle heart recover—"

"Okay, okay," I said, waving my hand. "Get over yourself."

He leapt up with a wicked grin, made himself a pot of coffee, put on a truly awful and unseasonable Christmas sweater, and headed Downstairs with me to map out what was down there.

Except we couldn't.

We'd grabbed flashlights in case of dark corners or burnt-out bulbs, but didn't need them. Every hall was lit by those cheerful bright wall sconces, and most of the rooms had a single bare bulb in the center of the ceiling. But it was the damnedest thing. We couldn't find an end to the place. We picked one hallway and wandered around for maybe fifteen minutes, through T-junctions and ninety-degree corners, past dozens of doors and half-furnished rooms. The same wood-paneled walls, seventies carpet, and wall sconces were everywhere. Downstairs was aggressively bland but disturbingly unbounded. It went from weird to surreal to sort of frightening, how much of it there was.

I'd poked my head into a room with an enormous old bureau— empty, like all the furniture—and a nook at the far end, a wooden dowel running along the top—like a doorless closet, maybe. I wandered over to investigate, hoping for a few dusty hangers, the remnants of an old calendar, some comforting sign of former human occupation. No such luck.

I mean, the place looked like people should have lived there, but aging furniture aside, there was almost nothing around to prove it. Anonymous marks scuffed the walls, the odd piece of lint dotted the floor, but there were no height marks penciled on door frames, no piles of old magazines, no bright squares on dirty walls where pictures once hung. Not a single old candy wrapper or forgotten sock. I ran my hand across the wooden dowel and wondered who had put it there, if anyone had ever hung clothes from it.

I turned around and saw Niko hadn't followed me in. I felt a moment of disorientation. The door seemed a long way away.

No—blinking, I realized it wasn't that. When I'd turned back toward the doorway, it wasn't there.

I frowned. The doorway was on the other side of the room from the one I'd instinctively turned to. I thought I'd walked along the wall to get to the nook, that it and the door had been on the same side. But the door was on the opposite wall, diagonally across from me.

I closed my eyes, suddenly dizzy. I remembered keeping the faded white wall to my right as I crossed the carpet to the closet nook. But when I looked again, the door was still where it was, in the opposite corner.

Obviously it hadn't moved.

You're doing it again.

Don't see things that aren't there. You fucking idiot.

Pushing away the uneasiness, I crossed diagonally across the carpet to the door, unable as I did to shake the sensation that I was tracing a different path than the one I'd walked coming in.

That this door led somewhere else.

I pushed my head out into the hallway. It looked just the same. Of course, they all did.

"Niko?"

No answer.

Okay, that's fine, I thought, keeping a firm grip on myself. I walked down the hall in the direction we'd been headed, peeked around the corner.

More hall, more carpet, more doors. No Niko.

I shouted his name again, louder.

Nothing.

It was so quiet.

I started down the hall, then halfway down thought maybe I should go back, not forward; then stopped in confusion. If you're lost you're supposed to stay put, not wander around.

The knob on the nearest door started to turn.

My heart tried to jump out my throat. The door thumped. The knob turned the other way, faster, more violent.

With a shuddery squeal the door burst open, Niko's shoulder leading the rest of him out.

"Stuck," he said, jiggling the knob. "Oh, goddammit. I spilled my coffee."

We looked down at the new dark stain on the carpet. He licked droplets from his fingers, inspected a candy-caned sweater cuff. "Thank Christ it didn't stain the cashmere."

"That is *not* cashmere," I said, rolling my eyes. "Hey. Don't wander off on me like that."

I didn't want to admit how spooked I'd been, and thought I'd done a good job hiding it, but of course he knew me better than that. He stared into me and seeing those emerald eyes full of concern was enough to melt my fear, transmute it into something infinitely better.

"Okay," I laughed. "You're not in trouble. Just stay close, yeah?"

"Sure, and sorry, but hey." His eyes had a mischievous glint. "Come check it out. I found stairs."

The new stairs led down into darkness. From the top we could see about twenty or thirty steps before things got shadowy, and enough of the shadows to tell the stairs kept descending for a while after that.

Niko had been excited to show me, but now he perched uneasily on the top step. I got out my flashlight and switched it on, pointing down. "Come on. Maybe there's some answers down there." He still looked hesitant. I put on my straightest face and my best P.I. voice. "Don't you want to get... to the bottom of this?"

"Mmm." He frowned in concern. "I just wouldn't want your boyfriend to get jealous, me spending all this time down here with you."

This was a little joke of his. I didn't have a boyfriend.

But he flicked on his own light, waved me on. "After you, amigo."

There were about eighty steps. Other than that, and the fact that we were lighting our way with flashlights, they seemed like any other stairs in a house built during the Carter administration and sinking into senility. That same damn carpet. They must have bought up the whole factory.

The wall sconces were still there, but no longer lit. Still no light switches anywhere.

When the stairs finally gave out, it was into another hallway, nearly identical to the ones above. This one felt a bit bigger, and the carpet a darker shade, looking more brown now, though maybe both impressions were a trick of the flashlights. Funny how much light influences your perception of spaces, of shapes. Colors. Everything, really.

More rooms opened off this hall, though these had more variety. A few doors were locked, which we hadn't encountered on the upper level. I searched the walls in vain for colored tacks with ripped corners of posters still attached, or even a crumpled gas station receipt. It wasn't like the place was sterile. Another room had a drain in the floor with stains running up to two big utility hookups on the wall, and the faint smells of dust and moths and yellowing wallpaper glue were everywhere. What was missing was anything personal.

The weirdest room, though, was the kitchen. It was too big for a kitchen, for starters, and had too much stuff in it: too many oven hookups, too much haphazard ceiling ventilation, red-handled water valves everywhere, and a dozen jumbled stove tops with holes where the burners should be. There were parts of appliances but no whole ones: bundles of wiring, even a kitchen sink. Niko tried the faucet and we both were startled when water came out. It was like a half-assembled restaurant kitchen with all the equipment jumbled together, rather than a row of stoves here, a row of dishwashers there.

I found what was clearly the plumbing for a toilet hookup in the middle of one wall, and had to put my foot down about this making any sense at all.

"Maybe a wall was supposed to go up here?" Niko shined his light between the bathroom plumbing and the nearest stovetop, but the kitchen stuff extended to either side.

"Who puts a toilet in the middle of a kitchen?" I didn't get it. He shrugged.

Just the one door, too, and nothing nearby that might have been a dining room or pantry, though we did find a large, empty, low-ceilinged room a few doors down. "Not that you could get a dining table down here," Niko mused. Same brown carpet, but no signs of anything to explain the room's purpose: no ceiling bulb or place to attach one, not even a single electrical outlet.

"You get the feeling whoever built this place didn't exactly know a lot about architecture?" Niko's voice was hushed in a kind of reverence. "Everything down here's off, you know? Like, who was that old lady in California who built that house with all the doors that went nowhere and fake hallways and everything?"

Sarah Winchester. I told him. Except her house is now an internationally famous tourist attraction. And this place was bigger.

Someone should have known about this.

Niko was thinking along the same lines. "Seriously, though. Who the fuck built all this? And why? For what?"

"No clue. But if there's any explanation, it's probably down here somewhere." I even half-believed that, which felt nice.

"I feel weird walking around a crazy person's house." His eyes darted around the empty room. "Not that I expect, like, pit traps and rotating blades. But it feels sort of... unsafe."

He kept glancing at me like he wanted me to say something that would make him feel better, to save him, so I tried my best like always. "You ever notice old horror movies have lots of really improbable architecture?" I babbled. "I want to meet some of those architects. Probably all dead now but I still want to grab them by their ghostly lapels and ask why the fuck they built all those crawlspaces and secret torture rooms and basements without proper lighting."

"You're freaking me out, man," Niko said. He held the light under his face, washing it out to a ghostly tan as his eyes rolled up into his head. "Vreeaking meee owwwwt."

"Attractive."

"You would totally date zombie me. Rotting flesh and all. Don't pretend you wouldn't."

"You're half-skeleton already. There's barely any flesh to rot off you."

"Come on." He grabbed my shoulder and propelled me down the hall. "Let's keep going." The rough of his hand shocked some courage back into me. My shoulder felt cool when he took the hand away.

A few more paces down the hallway, it opened into an octagonal room, a closed door in each wall other than the one we'd entered through. We tried a few. Each door opened onto another staircase leading down.

"But *seriously*," Niko said, alarmed. "This cannot possibly be here. It doesn't make sense." He looked towards me, desperate. "Ryan, help."

"Okay," I said, grasping at straws. "Maybe it's like a whole underground network. All the houses in the neighborhood connected together. People used to smuggle drugs or something. Underground railroad."

"Decor's too new," he countered. "And we haven't found any other stairs back up."

"Bomb shelter. Last owner decided to modernize. Dreamt of turning it into the ultimate student housing complex. Collapsed from construction debt before he could get rich off desperate kids willing to live in windowless asbestos-lined death traps."

He shook his head. "Let's go back, man. I don't like this. Something's not right."

I peered down one of the dark stairwells, frustrated. It bothered me that we might be so close to figuring this out. The next door might open onto something that explained it all.

And an undercurrent of excitement cut through the tinge of fear. This was fun. We were exploring. On a quest together.

I didn't want it to end.

"It can't go on forever," I said. "And whatever's deepest down will be most interesting, right?"

I talked him into it. After all there was nothing dangerous down here: it wasn't like exploring an abandoned mine shaft. Everything was in perfect repair even if no one seemed to have been here for years.

Big as it was, it was only architecture.

The staircase we picked dropped down for a few dozen steps, then turned at a weird angle and dropped some more. It wasn't necessarily smaller but felt more claustrophobic. Maybe that was my brain reminding me how deep underground we must be getting. At most of the landings a new hall branched off, each at a different angle. We kept going down.

After four or five weird angled twists the stairs ended, opening up into another corridor. Everything felt exactly the same, despite being stories deeper underground. It was as bland and anonymous as office space in a skyscraper.

There were more doors.

We shuffled past them, flashlights glinting off doorknobs and—*there* was a difference—instead of the wall sconces, fake candelabra now. You know the ones, with those awful faux-candles that flicker orange and don't fool anyone? They weren't lit now, anyway.

We stopped less to try side doors now, eager to get to the end of the hall, or the end of something, at least. Find some answers.

For a long stretch there were no doors at all, just wood paneling, so that when we did come to another door it was a relief, like exhaling held breath. Niko tried it, and it swung open onto a room unlike anything we'd seen so far.

It was concrete and tall, with rounded corners at the bottom. The ceiling was higher than the walls, like we were in a pit dug into a bigger room. In the center of the concrete floor was a drain.

Niko, intrigued, grabbed the bottom of a short ladder that ended around shoulder-height and pulled himself up to the top of the pit, flashlight swinging wildly. I clung to mine, keeping it steady like a candle I was afraid would blow out.

I felt afraid, without knowing why.

He shined his light back down at me. "Yep," he said, "it's a swimming pool."

That made sense, by some incredibly loose definition. "What's up there?"

He turned away from the lip, moved out of sight. Patterns of light swam across the ceiling as he swung the flashlight around. Something rattled. "Another kitchen." His voice bounced oddly off the rounded concrete. "This one's all furnished, though."

I was getting more and more unsettled, unaccountably so. "Any more doors?"

The reflections of light moved to and fro, like something alive. "Nope. No way in or out except through the pool. And there's no place to sit and eat, either." He paused. More scuffling. "Funny. The fridge is locked. Like, there's a keyhole on the fridge and you can't open it. Who does that?"

The door we'd come through, I noticed, was the same as all the others: cheap particle board, regular brass-plated knob. Not especially waterproof. I bent down, pushed it shut. Sure enough, there was a gap between it and the top of the carpet outside. Like you'd expect for any regular door not, you know, at the bottom of a swimming pool.

"Hey, Niko?" I straightened up, keeping my voice steady. "Let's go back." I wanted to add *I don't like this* or maybe *I want to get the hell out of here right now*, but some irrational fear gripped me that if I showed any weakness, he'd be the one who wanted to keep going down.

Going deeper.

Something rattled up there, wood scraping wood. "There's silverware in these drawers," he called, as if he hadn't heard me. "Cups in the cabinets too. Super seventies."

His voice was starting to seem unreal. I felt how tenuous a connection I had to him: a voice, the glints of his flashlight on the ceiling above the empty pool. Echoes and shadows. The distance between us seemed vast and growing vaster, maybe already unbridgeable.

And then. Maybe I imagined this, between the weird echoes of that concrete pool bottom and the nerves I'd worked up. But I thought I heard muffled voices. Faint. Coming through the wall.

Coming from the other side of the closed door back.

≫ 3 ≪

"Nikolaos," I hissed, trying to be loud and quiet at the same time and stumbling away from the door. "Get back down here, right now!"

He must have heard something in my voice, because seconds later his head poked over the edge, and he slid down the ladder and dropped the last few feet onto concrete. I could see him, I could suddenly even smell him, and that tangible reality felt overwhelmingly reassuring. I grabbed his arm and even his awful not-cashmere sweater was comforting.

"What's up?"

"I thought..." The noise had gone; I felt foolish. "I heard someone out there."

He walked to the door, pulling away from me. "No don't!" I hissed, but his hand was already on the knob, he was already turning it, pushing the door open, stepping out into the hallway. Shining his light left, back the way we'd come. He turned, to shine it to the right.

And for an instant I was sure

something

around the corner was going to grab him and in the same instant with nightmarelogic certainty I knew it was my fault for imagining it

for making it real

but nothing happened. He shrugged.

"I don't hear anything, man."

Neither did I.

"Let's get back anyway," he said. "We've been down here too long. Your boyfriend's going to kill me."

As we walked back up the hall through the zone without doors, I looked back. I noticed with a frown we'd left the door to the pool room open.

It felt wrong, somehow. A bad omen.

But no way in hell was I walking back to shut it.

We lay on my closed-again bed and stared up at the ceiling, giggling. We couldn't help ourselves. It felt good to be out of there, to have the whole ridiculous mystery literally at our backs. Even an old mattress felt like shield enough.

I'd felt better with each upward step. The earlier rooms were familiar as we hit them in reverse: the octagon with its stairs down, the bright yellow light of the upper halls, Niko's coffee stain ("so typical," I told him, "you've marked this place with your distinctive musk") and the big empty room with its couches and piles of everyone's junk. By the time we'd climbed the final stairs to my room and swung the bed shut, we were giddy, flushed with excitement, brimming with explanations and theories.

"It must run under the whole neighborhood," Niko was saying. "Connect to other houses, or maybe it only used to. Maybe no one knows about it any more." He grinned. "Except us."

"It doesn't make sense," I was still protesting, but it felt more ridiculous than sinister. I shook my head, embarrassed by my freak-out earlier. I was spooking myself for no reason. If someone else was down there, wouldn't they have come to say hi?

Maybe they did.

I shook my head again. It was cool, and nothing was going to get in the way of that.

I did some legit research in the next few days. Our landlord stopped by to see how we were settling in and reassure us he'd fix the things he said he'd fix before we moved in, which he clearly wasn't going to fix. He was a younger guy with kind of a stoner vibe, on the whole not very plausible as a landlord. When I casually asked how he'd come to acquire a hundred-year-old house in a rather nice college town, he said he was trying to make a living off rental properties and we were the first students to move into this one. He mentioned he'd gotten a good deal on the house because of the maintenance it needed (embarrassed cough) and because the city sold it at auction and they "weren't allowed to play bidding games and shit" with it.

"So the city repossessed it or something? Do you know who owned it before?" I asked, practically exuding casual nonchalance.

"Been empty for a long time," he said. "Was filled up with a ton of junk. Had to cart it all away before listing it."

"Oh yeah? What kind of junk?"

"Just..." he twirled his hand in a vague circle. "Stuff. Old furniture, old paint, piles of bricks. Nothing valuable."

I didn't ask if he knew anything about a secret basement the size of a city block, because I was afraid our rent would go up.

Down at city hall I looked up the property history, which I'd hoped would be more interesting than the chemistry I should have been studying. The house had indeed been built about a hundred years earlier. The records were aggressively boring. Certainly nothing about enormous sub-basements or a fleet of mining vehicles. I even hunted through microfilm of the local paper for anything unusual the week of construction. No dice.

After that, the trail went a bit cold because I had another acne flare-up, a bad one, dropped out of a class instead of showing up to take the midterm and felt generally miserable about myself for a couple of days. I finally pulled myself together enough to get some groceries and refill the expired prescription on my acne cream. I was in the bathroom, rubbing it on my pockmarked face and thinking about how much I'd been lied to as a kid. *Oh, that'll clear up when you get older.* Also *You'll figure girls out eventually* and *There's someone out there for everyone.* Classics, all.

Niko popped his head around the corner. "Dude. Phone's for you." He blinked at me. "You realize when you do that, it looks like you're rubbing jizz all over your face."

I didn't really see it. The last thing I thought about when looking in the mirror was anything sexy.

He must have guessed what I'd been thinking, because he punched my shoulder. "Dude, get over yourself. You're not Quasimodo." He sighed. "We need to get you a boyfriend."

"Store was fresh out," I said, but grimly resolved to start wearing my pride bracelet out in public again. "Who's on the phone?"

"Some lady from the local history society? I thought she had the wrong number, but she asked for you by name."

I had in fact called the history society a few days earlier, and the voice on the phone was an elderly woman who breathlessly said she'd love to chat about the old houses in our neighborhood, and invited us over to the society office for a cup of tea. The office turned out to be her living room. We sat on a sun-faded couch sipping something tasteless while she fawned over us ("so *wonderful* to see young people take an interest in local history"). It was awkward. I asked if she knew anything interesting about our address or any people who used to live there. She wasn't familiar with the house, although the mayor had once lived on our street, she told us, and she thought most of the houses near there had been built around the same time. Flailing, I asked if she knew anything about tunnels or underground rooms around town. She spun a not-very-interesting story about how during Prohibition a local bootlegger had dug a tunnel that led from his basement all the way to a poplar in the neighbor's backyard—nearly fifty feet long. I smiled and nodded demurely until I found a way to excuse us.

Meanwhile Niko had been making excursions on his own. I

got kind of upset when he told me—I'd wanted it to be our thing, something we did together—but he said he'd come get me the instant he found anything interesting, and didn't make too big deal out of it. It really bothered me, though. I thought about going on my own too but it felt wrong without him there. I itched with overwhelming curiosity but also a certain dread that kicked my heartbeat up a notch when I thought about walking too far down those halls, those stairs. I told myself I was being stupid but my pulse didn't listen.

Niko spitballed the idea of making a map, but figured it would be tricky. "A lot of those angles are non-standard," he said. "Those funny twists on the stairs down from the octagon, right? They're more than ninety degrees but less than the next sensible unit—one thirty-five or whatever. I have a feeling if you measured them they'd be fractional. Like one twenty nine point two three eight three eight." He laughed. "Three eight three eight three eight three eight three—"

"Quit it."

He smirked. "Irrational."

Some of the halls sloped up or down, too, enough that you could feel it when you walked them. Keeping track of what level everything was on would add to the confusion. I dragged discussion back up to the bigger picture. "It has to be mostly running east, doesn't it? Because of the hill. That big stairway doesn't go down far enough to get under 12th Street."

"I don't know." He visualized with closed eyes for a moment, then shrugged and opened them, shaking his head. "Hard to keep a sense of direction down there. We'll bring a compass next trip. You think those new GPS things for hiking would work?"

"No, they need line of sight to the sky. We could leave bread-crumbs, like Hansel and Gretel."

"We might have to, if it's much bigger." His eyes widened. "Can you imagine getting lost? Like some estate agent's nightmare. 'My god, I'll never be able to replace all this carpet!'"

We had a party down there. By unspoken agreement, the housemates didn't advertise the extent of the place: I put police caution tape from the dollar store across all the doorways out of the big room, as a joke, though I suspected I wasn't really joking. It was fine if everyone just saw a chill basement hangout spot. Much levity was made from the fact that you had to climb in and out of my bed to get there, or to go back up and take a piss.

We brought down a foosball table, some Christmas lights, lots of booze, and the stereo. I protested that my record collection was for archival purposes, not playing at parties, but I was overruled. It was an okay turnout and everyone, for all the usual reasons, focused on getting good and drunk. My usual social ineptness kept me from truly enjoying myself. Some girl tried to hit on me; I was so startled by this I blurted "Actually, I'm gay," which was even more awkward out loud than it sounds written down, and she laughed noisily and commiserated about the tragic ironies of dating for a few embarrassing seconds before vanishing, and only too late did I think to ask what the hell had compelled her to talk to me in the first place, because certainly whatever it was had never worked on any guys.

Not that I'd figured out how to go to parties where guys who'd be interested would hang out, anyway. I hated dance clubs and the couple gay bars I'd stepped into had given me massive anxiety attacks; I still felt a rush of panic when I thought about walking through the door of the tiny LGBT center on campus, even after years of passing it on the way to classes. I'd always thought things would get easier in college. At my enormous high school there hadn't been a single out queer person my freshman year, and I'd had no intention of being the first. Not only because of crippling shyness, self-image issues, and fear for my actual life, but because I literally did not know how to come out. Ellen hadn't done it on national TV yet when I was in high school; Kevin Kline hadn't done it at the movies, let alone sultry-eyed Jake Gyllenhaal; not enough gay teens had been famously killed or killed themselves to inspire anyone to tell us It Gets Better. Gay people basically did not exist in my universe, and yet there was I, somehow, gay regardless. College was supposed to have been an improvement. But once I got there, I failed to blossom into a beautiful flower. Maybe I should have moved farther away, to an actual big city, rather than somewhere close by and familiar and still red-state as fuck: but the problem wasn't my environment, I came to realize, it was me. It wasn't that I had issues with being gay: the internet had given me plenty of opportunities to come to terms and feel okay about it. I just didn't know how to be it in public, with other people, on any level but especially a romantic one, especially after what had happened in high school.

Meanwhile the straight people were having a nice party. Niko, wearing a blue bowling shirt with "My Name is BONG" stitched into the lapel and a pair of tight-fitting lime-green jeans, whose only virtue was the tight-fitting part, was shadowing some girl he'd been trying to hit it off with. It wasn't going well. They got into an argument early in the evening (Dear LiveJournal: I tune out when I hear the phrase "That's *not* what Marx said") and she stormed off up the stairs. Niko fumed, then stormed off himself, reappearing minutes later in a Linkin Park t-shirt and torn jeans and carrying a bottle of tequila, which he used like a police baton to corral me into a corner to do shots with him.

"Said I dress too fucking weird for her," he said with a hollow Ashes to Ashes sort of intonation. "Is *this* fucking normal enough? Whatever. The hell with everyone." I could drink to that. We threw back a shot, sitting on the carpet with our backs to the paneled wall. Niko was always swinging between extremes: at high ebbs he wanted to be friends with everyone, at low ebbs I was the only person in the universe. He was busy furiously ignoring the rest of the party, which I wasn't feeling much connection to either.

He sniffed. "You know when we first moved over here I didn't speak any English?" I nodded; I'd heard this story before. "My parents thought it'd be cute to dump me into third grade like that. You know, *full immersion.*" His face twisted.

I poured him another shot, thinking I probably shouldn't, but by then I already had.

He leaned back against the wall, looking worn down. "I tried so fucking hard to fit in. To get to where just opening my mouth didn't mark me out as a freak. By the time junior high started none of the new kids even knew. Master fucking performance." He tugged at the t-shirt, a corner of his mouth twitching. "Meanwhile the fam all expects things to be exactly like we'd never left. Like America's just a little rest stop, like of course I'll want to go back to Greece and have a million kids as soon as I graduate. My aunt asked me at Thanksgiving why I wasn't married yet. I reminded her I am twenty-two years old and still in the middle of fucking college." He sipped at the shot, winced. "Urgh. Never sip tequila." He held it up to the light, squinted suspiciously. "Anyway. She said neither of those things stopped my uncle."

I was staring idly at a dark-haired girl and a bearded jock flirting on the couch across the room, words swallowed up by the thumping of the stereo. Thinking about the music echoing down all those empty halls. "I can't even imagine getting married."

"Yeah, neither can the government."

"Not just that, asshole." I side-kicked him, then frowned, trying to figure out what I wanted to say. "I don't know. I can't imagine anyone wanting to spend the rest of their life with me. Or that I could believe someone would say yes, if I wanted to with them."

I closed my mouth, feeling stupid, but he was nodding. "Yeah, I dig you. Thinking you could be that for someone. Believing in yourself that much." He was frowning. "I can't believe in anything they fucking want me to be."

He tilted his head back, eyes closed. "Well, you ever make it there, you got a best man lined up at least." He opened one skeptical eye. "Or are there two best men? How would all that even work?"

"I don't know." I closed my eyes, too. *Dear LiveJournal. Figure out how all that even works.*

We listened to the music for a minute, surrounded by people who naturally knew how to Saturday night, without training. It was kind of nice being near them, at least.

Niko said, very quiet: "Can't get married till you go on at least one date."

"Thanks," I said. "Good tip."

"For reals, though. You need to put yourself out there, man. Get over whatever hang-ups you got going on."

"New topic." I moved to pour myself another shot. He grabbed the bottle, held it out of reach.

"Nuh uh. Confession time. I went, now it's your turn."

"Fuck you."

"Seriously, man." He sat up straighter, fixed me with that look that told me I wasn't getting it. "I know you've dated before. In high school, right? Wasn't his name Brandon or something?"

"Bradley," I said against my will, something inside me deflating. I still didn't want to tell him, but realized I was going to.

"So what happened? Bad breakup?"

I closed my eyes, not wanting to rip open these scabs. Not on a Saturday night I'd almost been enjoying.

"I broke up with him," I said quietly, but it was enough for it all to start coming out. "Yeah, okay. The story. So I knew him from band, and he cornered me after practice one day. Someone told him I was into weird old music too. He's got all these bizarro cross-genre mix tapes in his backpack, pulls some out to play for me. Adorable. We hung out in the band room listening to them for hours after everyone else had gone home."

I sighed. "It took me a while to figure out the signals he was sending because I had no idea how to, like, receive them. But we figured it out in the end. It was, you know. All that first love stuff. Sneaking out at midnight. Lots of giggling. It was amazing. At first."

"Uh oh." Niko slouched back down, settling in for the long haul.

I tried to keep talking even though I could feel myself clenching up, chest muscles trembling. "It just became apparent pretty quick that he was way, way more into me than I was into him. He *loved* me with every part of himself"—I could feel Niko's eyebrows waggling but I pressed on, knew I couldn't stop the story now—"and it was so fierce it was... like being burned. It *hurt*, that I couldn't love him back like that. I didn't know how to take it. And then one day at lunch in the cafeteria I was going to break up with him and I think he sensed it coming, wanted to stop it. So he—oh god." I closed my eyes and, yup, there they were: moisture squeezed out between them. "We weren't out, you know. In our town. At our school especially. Nobody was. He stands up on the table, little Bradley Thompson, shouts for attention, shouts in a louder voice than I'd ever heard him use that we're in love, that we didn't care who knew it, that our love would last forever and nobody in the universe could stop it."

"Shit," Niko breathed.

I took a quick breath. "I don't really remember the rest of that day. I know we got sent to the principal's office because that's where my mom picked me up from. There were adults in the cafeteria so I don't think anyone tried anything, but I'm sure the reaction would have been... laughter. Disgust. Thrown banana peels. Maybe some kids would have thought about stopping it, standing up, supporting us, but I doubt anyone actually did, would have dared. But I don't remember. It's all blank. Just... the aftermath."

"Yeah?"

"We broke up," I said, "and I want to talk about that part even less." I pulled the bottle out of his loose fingers and finally poured the shot, downed it.

"That is the worst coming out story I've ever heard."

"Not really." I shrugged. "I didn't get kicked out of my house. Didn't get sent to the emergency room. Guess that was probably when I started drinking, though. I was a good kid before that."

"You've always been a good kid," he said, managing not to make it sound like an insult. "So look, just so you know. Dating is generally speaking a lot better than that."

"So I hear." My mood was bottoming out into pitch-black despondency. "Haven't really worked up the enthusiasm to find out, though."

From the corner of my eye I could see him looking at me, the flashing Christmas lights lost in his black curls, more swallowed up than reflected by them. He seemed fragile in the shifting light. Sharp, but delicate. Able to be shattered. I knew he was trying to think of something encouraging to say and all at once I couldn't stand the thought.

I pushed out words. "Can we just, like. Not talk any more."

"No problemo." He slumped back against the wall. But he leaned into me, just a little. I leaned into him, too.

We stayed like that for a few minutes.

Then some friends of his tromped down the stairs and he leapt up, pulling a sparkling smile and manic laugh out from somewhere, pouring drinks and giving high fives, and dragged me with him into the noise, and one of his friends talked me into getting trounced at foosball, and everyone kept drinking. And the moment between us faded into ephemera and lost any possible significance, even to me.

Not long after, Niko disappeared. I figured maybe he'd gone back to his room to be alone: despite appearances, his social energy was limited, had to be rationed. I didn't think anything of it, focused on getting drunk with everyone else because it seemed like the thing to do.

Midnight passed, unnoticed.

Some time later the party started winding down. Soon it had winnowed to a couple hardcore foosballers, the girl and the beardy dude making out on the couch, and a few sozzled, earnest conversations in corners. I extracted myself from one of these, but on my way upstairs to take a leak I noticed that the flashlight we'd left by the hall—the one that led to the octagon room, the long stairs, and the pool—was gone.

Had he gone exploring? Tonight?

If he had, he'd been gone a long time.

An hour later the party had just about wrapped. Still no sign of Niko. I'd checked his bedroom—empty—and polled a few housemates. No one had seen him since the start of the night. I felt a stab of guilt for getting so wasted, for not looking out for him; pushed down vague resentments at feeling like I had to.

I was standing at the hallway wondering if I should go look for him, when a shadow appeared at its end and my body tried to jump out of my skin.

It was him, of course. But my relief only lasted for a second. As he got closer, a prickling sense crept into my bones that something was wrong.

He was stepping carefully, like over ice, deliberate, head turned down to the carpet. For a moment I wasn't sure it was him at all.

He noticed me, gave me the thinnest of smiles. Sweat beaded on his face, which was ashen, like he'd been throwing up. He grabbed my arm as if to keep from falling over. His hand was cold.

"You okay?" I asked.

He nodded. "Yeah. Just need to go to bed."

"Did you—" I wanted to say *see something down there*, but couldn't quite work up the nerve. "—have too much to drink or something?"

He chuckled, weak. "Bed." He brushed passed me, and headed, wobbly, up the stairs.

$$\gtrapprox 4 \lessapprox$$

After that everything changed. He'd lost all interest in Downstairs. If I brought it up he'd change the subject; if folks were hanging out down there he wouldn't come. When I finally asked him directly about this, he shook his head.

"I don't think it's a good idea to be down there, that's all." He tried to play it off casual, but his jaw was set.

Something about him had changed. His wardrobe turned straight-laced. He went back to calling himself Nick. He watched a lot of sports on TV. And things were strange between us. Our conversations didn't go quite right, didn't fit in their familiar grooves. We'd get derailed, trail off. We started talking less. I couldn't point to something specific that had changed, but the usual pleasurable tension between us, the taut bond of connection we'd had since the accident, was gone. He didn't seem to need me any more. He seemed like just a dude. Just a Nick. Not mine.

I worked up my courage and did a few of my own solo expeditions Downstairs, without telling him, but I couldn't convince myself to go very far. I hallucinated strange noises around corners: floorboards creaking, whispered sighs. I knew I was only scaring myself, but didn't have it in me to stay down there for long.

I lay on my bed a lot and listened to records through my headphones. My dad's old headphones: huge bulky black things with a coiled cord like old telephones. Sometimes I held my breath while I did it. This was an old technique of mine to shut the world out. After a while outside sounds would slip away, and the thrum of blood and music would fill my ears, become my entire universe. As a kid I could hold my breath for three minutes. Enough sometimes to make it through a whole song without breathing.

I fell asleep one night doing this, headphones on, and dreamed about Niko, which happened now and then whether I wanted it to or not. In the dream I was at the hallway junction again, looking down into the shadows at the figure at its end. Only this time it wasn't me down there, it was him, walking toward me. Not hesitant but confident, smiling, happy to see me. I grinned back, thrilling at the reciprocity between us, a bond that felt in that moment tinged with something else, something more primal.

But then I faltered, because I realized I wasn't sure quite what that meant. There are a lot of primal emotions.

There were so many things that smile could mean.

I took a step back, afraid, but there was nothing but empty space behind me. I was standing at the lip of a drop-off.

He came right up to me, Niko, my Niko, looking into my eyes with something I was certain now was love, and the fear faded as he reached up to touch my cheek, and the warmth of it and the smell of him and the look on his face fused inside me into need so intense it parted my lips, as if for oxygen, just as he bent down with hunger to kiss them.

It was a beatific kiss, velvet, brain-melting, the kind you sometimes get in real life if you're lucky but I'd only ever had in dreams, sweet and lingering and seraphic. Everything I'd ever wanted flowed through me into him and I imagined I could feel the same from him to me, echoed and amplified, conjoined. It went on and on and on. He pressed against me, arms wrapped around my back, holding me, and mine were maybe around him too but only limply, subconscious, the kiss and its indescribable tangibility, its dream-forgotten trueness the only thing, the only thing. The only thing.

It wasn't until I'd broken it, pulled back to look up at him, that I realized I was leaning back over the edge behind me, his arms holding me there, my toes the only thing still touching the lip of the drop-off.

I couldn't read his expression. Had no idea what it meant at all.

I didn't even know who he was.

He let me fall.

I plummeted down into darkness, gathering speed, faster and faster. I'd had dreams before that ended like this, a sickening fall and then an ejection back to wakefulness right as I hit ground, covered in cold sweat and shuddering. But this time when I woke, it was more like I'd chosen to do it, pulled away from the dream against its will. Like part of me knew if I'd stayed I'd have kept falling forever, because there was no ground down there to stop me.

The record was turning in its final groove. I stared at it dumbly, dad's big headphones still muffling the outside world, transmitting only hissing, clicks and pops.

This has got to stop, I told myself, *you're over him. You got over him a long time ago.* The accident had confused everything but in the months after it I'd sorted myself out, realized it was never going to happen. Put it away and moved on. I had. It was just my fucking dreams didn't seem to have gotten the memo.

I felt Downstairs tingling at my back, beneath me. I switched the player off and took my blanket to sleep on the couch in the living room.

One night not long after that, everyone but Niko and I went out to a concert. We started drinking, and it seemed to ease the friction between us, which made us both want to keep drinking. I found comfort in this, maybe the first acknowledgment that he felt the gap between us too, wanted as much as me to find a way to close it.

Deep into a bottle of vodka, we got into one of those hilarious drunken arguments about nothing: the final line to one of our favorite movies. I was sure it was one thing, he was sure it was something a few words off. I knew I was right, and also could see why he might remember it wrong, but he refused to believe me. He tried to pull out his cell phone to call a friend for a second opinion and got it stuck on something in his pocket: laughing, he ended up dumping everything out on the table, but then we got distracted by a text he'd gotten from an ex-girlfriend, which led to more drinking and another argument where I dutifully tried to keep him from responding, not just because he was drunk but because back then with those flip phones it would have taken him a fucking hour to peck out a reply.

We ended up slumped in our chairs, the vodka bottle empty, listening to some spacey ambient music on the stereo.

"Niko," I said, or maybe the vodka said it for me. "The other night. At the party."

"What about it?" he muttered, eyes closed.

I couldn't say what I wanted to say. Words come easy until you find the ones that won't come at all, that could shatter un-examined concords in seconds, weaken load-bearing truths. We have universes in our heads that we live in, and the wrong words puncture them, burn them up like airships filled with something unspeakably combustible but embarrassingly common. Dear LiveJournal: Oh, the humanity.

Even the vodka couldn't figure out how to navigate all that. I stayed silent for a long time, until I heard Niko gently snoring. Too late, again, as always. I hadn't yet found the right headspace for this conversation, was perpetually too sober to start it or too drunk to finish.

I started to drift off myself, but then shook myself awake. Niko was out cold. Before I could wake him and convince him to drag himself to bed I noticed something out of the corner of my eye.

In the pile of stuff he'd pulled from his pocket (phone, wallet, keys, crumpled receipts) were two small brass keys.

They weren't on his keyring, just loose in his pocket, and faintly corroded with age.

It was hard to tell for sure, but they looked identical.

Nothing about this was all that unusual but somehow I knew one of those keys would fit the fridge Downstairs. Don't ask how I knew this, because I couldn't tell you, but I did. Irrational.

That ridiculous locked fridge in that ridiculous kitchen atop a ridiculous empty pool.

He'd been keeping something from me.

Had he found something in there?

Something that scared him off going back?

What inside a fridge could be that scary? Could make him lie to his best friend?

I'm not sure why I did it. The vodka, maybe. Repressed curiosity. Or maybe the growing frustration that something had happened to Niko, something had changed; but I wasn't allowed to know what it was, or ever put it right.

Quietly, I took the keys. I shouldn't have, but by then I already had.

The house was dead quiet, which made the transition to Downstairs feel even more natural. Despite my earlier trepidations, I wasn't afraid as I grabbed the flashlight by the hallway. Vodka is magic.

I passed through the first few hallways, the stairs where the lights went out, the dark lower corridors. It wasn't until I hit the octagon that I got scared again.

I'd been walking on autopilot, lost in musing, but as I stepped into that room with its stairs leading down, I pulled up short, noticing something vital. The flashlight was dimmer. My eyes had adjusted, but through my liquor-addled head I noticed the room was still less bright than the last time I'd been down here. Niko must have run down the batteries with all his exploring. This didn't especially worry me: after our first trip I'd brought up this possibility. "Yeah, fuck that," he'd said, and duct-taped four fresh batteries to the long body of the flashlight.

But it did occur to me—now—that to change them down here I'd have to do it in total darkness. Fiddling with sticky tape, fumbling to unscrew the light, pouring out the old batteries and not mixing them up with the new ones, by feel...

So there was that.

I thought for a minute about going back. But I was close to the pool room now. I wanted to find out what was inside that fridge. What Niko had been keeping from me.

And I did have the batteries, after all. If I needed to change them, it would just take a second.

I kept going.

The last set of stairs down, with their weird irrational angles, passed quickly. The hall at the bottom stretched into the gloom, and I sped past the long stretch with no doors till I reached the pool room.

The door was closed. So Niko *had* been back here.

Inside was the smooth curved concrete of the pool bottom. I grabbed for the lowest rung of the ladder and pulled myself up, a familiar motion from my swimming days made unfamiliar through lack of buoyancy, being clothed and bone-dry.

The upper level had a lip about three feet wide extending around the edge of the empty pool, and on the ladder side the space opened up, concrete giving way to linoleum. Sure enough, there was a full kitchen up there, just like Niko had described. With all the appliances, it was fairly cozy. I stared bemused at the chrome dials on the oven, the row of pale-green cabinets with round white handles.

I turned to the fridge. It looked dated, a fading yellow with tacky chrome highlights. It only had one big door; no freezer. No magnets or family photos, either. Generically anonymous.

I pulled at the handle, but it didn't budge. Studying it, I saw what Niko had been talking about: there was a small keyhole under the handle. Smaller than a house key: more like one for a padlock, something you'd put on a shed.

The keys I'd lifted from Niko looked about right.

I picked one and slid it into the lock. It went in smooth, with a satisfying click as it bottomed out. But when I turned it, it wouldn't rotate.

Frustrated, I jigged it back and forth, turning harder. The key was too small to get a solid grip on. I squeezed down and gave it a really good twist.

For a second I thought it was turning, but then I realized I'd bent the key. I'd come close to snapping it in half.

I pulled it gingerly from the lock, staring at it in disappointment. Well, shit. There wouldn't be any hiding this from him now. It was bent nearly in half. I slipped it into my back pocket as I tried to think what to do.

In between the little noises I made, the taps and scratches and breaths, the silence almost smothered me.

Try the other key.

It slid in easy too, and when I gently twisted this one, it turned. I rotated it through a full three sixty before I heard a second snick.

I pulled at the fridge handle and the door swung open, cold air and yellow light wafting out.

I wasn't sure what I expected to see (*frozen heads*, the part of my brain still traumatized by horror movies suggested) so it took a moment of blinking in confusion to realize the fridge was empty. There weren't even any shelves other than the one above the crisper drawers on the bottom, though the walls had notches where they should go. But no food. A butter dish and condiment nooks in the door, unused.

There was nothing in there.

Except—frowning, I bent down, shining the light inside. The fridge was *deep*. It went back a good six feet. And there was something on the back wall.

The inside of another fridge door. Condiment nooks. Another butter dish.

What the hell?

Feeling foolish, I clambered inside, flashlight bumping against the plastic floor above two pairs of crisper drawers, one facing in, one facing out. They held my weight.

I shuffled forward, hunched over (there was less than five feet of vertical space) and pushed the inner door. No give. I pushed harder, remembering stories about kids stuck in fridges, but still nothing. *Is this one locked too?* I searched for a keyhole, but didn't see one. *Which makes sense, if it's on the outside.* I turned back to confirm: yep, the door I'd come through had no sign of a lock on its inner surface.

The logo on the plastic butter compartment said Whirlpool.

A thought popped into my head: *What if it's like an airlock?* This made no kind of logical sense, but seemed compelling. Only one door open at a time, otherwise you'd let all the cold air out. I almost giggled, then stopped myself, afraid.

What am I doing?

I decided to try it. Turning awkwardly, I reached for the door I'd come through with the hand holding the flashlight to pull it shut. It wasn't designed to be pulled from the inside, but I got a grip on a condiment shelf and swung it firmly towards me.

As the door slammed shut two things happened, both terrifying in different ways. First, there were two snicks, one from the door in front of me and one behind.

Second, I lost my grip on the flashlight, and it tumbled out of my hands, hit the hard shelf underneath me with a crack, and went out.

Cold terror flushed through me. I felt for the light, grabbed it and shook it, pressed the button on and off. Nothing happened. I pushed the door in front of me but it didn't give at all. I slammed into it hard with my whole body, panicking, the rounded edge of a plastic shelf jabbing into my cheekbone, but the door didn't budge.

Because it's locked, I told myself, mind whirling. *But the one behind you is open, now.* I twisted around, facing the back of the fridge as near I could tell, the second door.

But the thought of opening that door in pitch blackness, a door leading into complete unknown, opening it blind and crawling out into darkness, was terrifying. I stayed frozen, caught between fears: staying there or moving forward. Finally some combination of claustrophobia and visions of my air running out triumphed over my fear of the unknown. Trying to keep my breathing calm, I unscrewed the end of the flashlight by feel, dumped out the old batteries, and one at a time replaced them with the fresh ones duct-taped to its sides. I held my breath and turned it on.

Blessed light flooded the tiny chamber.

Anxious to escape, I crab-walked forward till my outstretched hand touched the other door. Before I could stop to think, I kept moving forward, pushing my weight against it.

The door opened easily. Stumbling on cramped knees, I spilled out of the fridge and staggered upright, shining my light around warily. But what I saw confused me even more.

It was the same room.

I frowned, mind working, flashing the light over every surface like a brush that might paint sense into what I was seeing.

It was the same kitchen—same ovens, same green cabinets, same improbably-adjacent concrete pool. Not a mirror image, or a slightly different design: it was the same room I'd just left. The only difference was the fridge was on the opposite wall.

Like it had connected through the wall to an identical room on the other side.

Dizzy.

I took a few steps forward, shined the light over the edge of the pool. Same ladder, same door, although it was shut. Had I shut it behind me this time? I'd been in a hurry. I couldn't remember.

I turned back to the fridge, and froze.

The door had swung shut behind me.

I pulled on the handle, but it didn't budge. Locked.

Shit. Where was the key? I'd left it in the lock on the other side. But the other one, the one I'd bent, the one that didn't fit, was still in my pocket.

I pulled it out again to frown at it, knowing somehow what would happen before I tried it. Sure enough, when I slipped the bent key into the lock and turned it, this time it rotated easily and the door swung open.

Different key. Different lock. *Different door.*

Different room.

I shut and locked it again, shaking my head.

I had to see. I climbed down the ladder, dropped onto the concrete. I opened the door onto the doorless hallway.

A wave of déjà vu hit me as I looked down it. It was the same hall I'd passed through minutes before—but I knew it couldn't be. I'd crawled out the other side of the fridge. This wasn't the same place, and yet it had that ineffable tang of familiar places, the twinge that tells you *I've been here before.*

As I walked down the hallway, I looked for some distinguishing feature to confirm this intuition: but the decor was, as always, so bland that nothing stood out. It could have been any basement hallway anywhere.

When I hit the stairs back up to the eight-sided room, though, something went wrong.

I'd stopped without meaning to, clutching the banister, foot on the first step. I looked up the stairs, and a faint twinge of vertigo brushed me. Or not vertigo, exactly. It's hard to describe.

It wasn't quite premonition, a sensation, a tingling, an insight. It wasn't like knowing or feeling at all.

Something inside me between emotion and intuition just didn't want to go back up there.

When Bradley had outed us both in high school the aftermath had been ugly, in more ways than one. My house started getting egged once or twice a week. Sometimes it was worse than eggs. One day I came home from school and someone had drawn a red chalk outline on our driveway, like at a murder scene. Next to it they'd written *your next queer*. I got the hose and a brush and scrubbed it out fast, wanting it gone before mom got home from work, because she'd already moved me to a new school and I was afraid if she saw the chalk outline, the message, she'd move us to a whole new state, have to quit her job and leave behind her friends and my sister's too, both of them giving up everything because of me, and I couldn't stand the thought of that. I think that was the first time I really understood that some people weren't just grossed out by gay people, or morally offended. They wanted us dead. That was how wrong they thought we were. To know just existing could make people feel that way about you, to realize that this was the world you'd have to live in, to keep growing up in. If you could.

The creeping feeling I felt now was like that. An existential wrongness. And it was getting stronger. Like a light from around a distant corner, growing brighter.

I listened, motionless, but heard nothing. The quiet pressed against me.

What am I going to do? Go back?

No.

Taking a deep breath, I made an impulsive decision. A few paces back was a door, and without stopping to think I pulled it open. The room inside was crammed with furniture under sheets. On a normal day this might have scared the piss out of me, but this feeling of wrongness was getting so strong I would have run straight into a room full of oversized spiders rather than stay in that hallway any longer.

I slipped in and shut the door behind me, quietly—that felt important—and ran to the far end of the room. Spotting something sofa-shaped, I lifted the edge of the sheet that covered it and half-crawled, half-dived inside. Flipping onto my back, I smoothed the sheet, held my hand over the flashlight—I couldn't bear to turn it off—and held my breath.

The feeling had diminished when I ran across the room, but now was growing again. I was trembling. I tried not to breathe, to relax my face as if doing so would open my ears wider, let me hear fainter sounds.

It was deathly quiet. All I could hear was my heartbeat.

The top of my hand glowed a dull red as the flashlight beam lit up bones and the dark veins between them.

The feeling reached an unbearable crescendo, and held there sustained. I was shivering and couldn't stop. It was a wrongness, wrongness on every level, filling up my body. I wanted it to go away more than anything.

I thought I heard something move in the hallway outside. Scuffing the carpet, maybe.

Then, mercifully, the feeling started to drain away.

I let out a breath, then took in another. With each one I felt more in balance, an equilibrium I'd never thought to appreciate until now. In another minute, all that was left was me: coated in sweat, crashing off adrenaline, but all right.

And yeah, it took fifteen minutes to muster the courage to lift the sheet and walk back across that room. Now that my regular instincts were back, the thought of what might be under all those other sheets was fucking terrifying.

When I'd recovered, I hurried across the room, out into the hall, and back up the stairs. My brain had gone numb: I let myself feel like I was retracing my steps, but another part of me knew I moved through different halls and rooms, on the wrong side of the fridge. But going back would mean following the direction that ugly feeling had drifted—and I couldn't do that. So I climbed the stairs to the octagon room, through the identical hallways back, and up the second stairs to the lighted upper levels, everything exactly as it should have been.

When I saw the coffee stain, though, I stopped.

It was right where Niko had spilled it on our first trip down, where the coffee had sloshed as he'd forced open the sticky door.

It was the same hallway. But I couldn't explain how.

What had happened? My brain whirred, trying to manufacture sense.

What I finally decided was this: I must have gotten turned around in the dark fridge. Banging the inside of the door, trying to force it open, I somehow moved the fridge, pushed it across the kitchen to the opposite wall. When I came out, it was through the other door, but into the same room. And I must have gotten confused about the keys: maybe I hadn't turned the first one the right way when I tried it, that was all.

I couldn't honestly convince myself of this.

It's the same coffee stain.

I felt superimposed. It had to be the same hallway, and yet it had to be a different one. This was the same stain, and yet I was a ten-minute walk from where Niko had spilled his coffee.

Maybe going Downstairs drunk had been a bad idea.

I kept going. I made it back to the big room, looking just as I'd left it, and climbed the final stairs gingerly. But my room was waiting for me at the top, nothing out of place: my records, my textbooks, my dirty laundry. That settled that. Somehow, I'd come back the same way I went in. But I felt deflated, unresolved, like the last fifty pages of the book had been left out. *And then he: The End.*

I shut the bed behind me more firmly than necessary. I considered nailing it shut but settled for piling some heavy boxes on top of it.

It had been maybe an hour since I'd left. Niko was still passed out on the couch in our front room.

I curled up on the next couch over and, despite being so keyed up I could barely think, dropped into sleep.

I woke some time later to Niko shaking my shoulder, and sat up, bleary-eyed. It was still dark outside.

"Go to bed," he was saying, "it's late."

I yawned. The trip Downstairs seemed like a dream, coming back in bits and pieces. I snuck a glance at the corner of the table where he'd emptied his pockets, but his stuff was gone. Did he notice I'd taken the keys?

Shit. I'd have to tell him.

"Hey man," I said, dreading this. "You remember earlier when you pulled your shit out to get your phone, and left it on the table?"

He blinked. "Um. No."

He'd been pretty drunk. I pressed on. "We were about halfway through finishing that bottle." The vodka bottle was about a quarter full. I frowned. Hadn't we killed it?

Shaking my head, I pressed on. "Look. What I'm trying to say is, I took the keys. I'm sorry. I just wanted to know if you'd found something down there. Why you hadn't told me. I went but there was nothing there, and I got turned around and... anyway, it doesn't matter. I screwed up and I lost one key, and uh, kind of damaged the other." It sounded so stupid as I said it, and I hated myself, both for stealing from him and for failing to discover anything useful with them. "I'm an idiot, man, and I'm sorry. But look, if you tell me where you found them, maybe we could figure something out, and talk about what's going on, and everything?"

Niko was frowning, but didn't seem angry. Maybe this wasn't going to be a big deal after all.

He sat down on the floor next to me, a serious look on his face.

"Orion," he said, "exactly what fucking keys are you talking about?"

≋ 5 ≋

We sat on the floor of the empty house, still miles from dawn, and each word we spoke brought us closer to panic.

Niko said he'd never found any keys. And as I tried to piece together the evening, to backtrace what had happened, little details kept failing to add up. The vodka bottle. The movie quote: now he agreed with me, was baffled that I thought he could possibly get it wrong. He pulled out his phone and showed me the last text from his ex: four months ago.

Despite these discrepancies, something felt right about the way we discussed them. We were back in sync again. The strained awkwardness and stunted conversations of the past week were gone. It felt like he'd been away on a trip and we were catching up again, despite the fact that we'd been seeing each other all week.

But when I told him where I'd been that night, about the fridge and the keys, it was like I'd punched him in the face.

He bolted up, took a few paces, then collapsed into a chair, stricken. "Oh, shit," he kept saying. "Oh shit oh shit oh shit."

He wouldn't say anything else until I poured him another shot of vodka—the vodka we'd already finished, goddammit—and then the story started breaking out of him in dangerous pieces.

"Okay, so. The night of the party." He looked drained. "I didn't feel like talking, you know, to other humans. So I went exploring. Had a vague thought like maybe I'd find something interesting to bring back up and show you." He ran a shaky hand through his kinked hair. "But something..." He swallowed. "Something happened, okay? And I got to the pool room and I couldn't go back the same way." He waved a hand at my raised eyebrow. "Let me just finish telling this, okay?"

He wouldn't say what had happened, but it made him change course, and eventually he found himself approaching the pool room door from the other direction. He climbed the ladder into the kitchen, but when he got there found the fridge not only unlocked, but open—the outer door, at least. He'd done the same thing I had: climbed inside, pulled the door shut, lost his light, pushed the other door open—and climbed out with the same spatial confusion I'd had.

I told him my theory about knocking the fridge around, but he shook his head. "No, I don't think so. When my light went out, I was pretty deliberate with my motions, exactly because I didn't want to get turned around. I barely jostled the thing. And there's something else that makes me think..."

He swallowed, licked his lips. For a long minute, he couldn't meet my eye. Then he grabbed my knee, as if to steady himself, looked over at me. Looked hard. "Ryan. Man. This is going to sound crazy. But listen, okay? This place. This house." He looked around furtively, as if we were someplace dangerous and not the living room of our college crash pad. "We're not where we used to be. *This is a different place.*"

"Step off," I said, rejecting this at once. "It's one thing to say there's a couple mirrored hallways down there, but there's not a whole different house up here. There aren't clones of our goddamn roommates, a different street and sky and..."

I trailed off, because he was staring at me, miserable. I realized this was exactly what he thought was happening.

"Look," I said, worried and afraid, "let's go back right now. I'll show you the coffee stain. That proves it."

"I'm not going back down there." He pulled back. "I've been

too damn terrified to even think about it, after what I..." He bit his lip, looked away. Took the last swig of vodka.

Tingles crawled down my neck. "What you saw? Well, what was it?"

He didn't answer for a while. I thought he was trying to remember at first, and then maybe that he was trying to forget.

Finally, defeated, he told me. "On my way down. Before I got there. I started feeling... off. Like something was wrong."

He stopped, trembling. Phantom insects crawled up my back. What did he see to rattle him this bad?

"That long hallway. Without any doors. I was walking down it, and I saw another light."

I sat rigid. "What the fuck?"

"I kept walking," he went on, not looking at me. "I didn't want to turn my back, get chased down. That sick feeling got stronger. Sharper. But I couldn't stop walking. Couldn't turn around."

He took a deep breath. "The light got closer. It was someone with a flashlight. They were walking toward me the same way I was walking toward them. I couldn't see their face. I just kept walking. I kind of hugged the right wall and they hugged the left. The flashlight was right in my face. I couldn't see anything until we were only a few steps apart."

He met my gaze at last, forehead wet with cold sweat, like he was reliving that queasy sensation. My own stomach twisted. I couldn't breathe.

"Ry," he said, "I passed myself. I walked right past another me with another flashlight, who looked as sick and fucked up as I did. And we both kept walking. We didn't stop. I made it to the pool room, climbed the ladder, and went right through that fucking fridge to get farther away. And there is no fucking way I'm going back down there again."

I swallowed. "Dude. It was dark. You were messed up. Maybe you saw someone else down there, but what you're saying, man.

It's impossible."

"Irrational." A hollow laugh. "Things are different here. On this side. I'll show you. What's the smallest bill you've got in your wallet?"

"Uh, I don't know." Taken aback, I pulled it out, riffled through the smaller bills. He smiled grimly at one of them, snatched it, held it up.

"Better hold onto this. Because no one here's ever heard of one."

"What are you talking about?" I said, annoyed.

And over the next hour, he showed me.

We pored through the dusty encyclopedia in our front foyer. We combed the magazines sitting in the house, dragged out Monopoly. We fired up the Internet (all GeoCities and tedium in those days) and found pictures of cash registers, government websites, coin collectors talking about the history of currency.

According to everything we could find, the US Government had never, at any point in its history, issued a three dollar bill as legal tender.

We stared at the one from my wallet with growing unease. Buchanan's familiar portrait stared back, implacable. Niko tapped the portrait's chin. "That right there might be the only one that exists in this place. Wherever we are."

We cobbled together a theory out of guesswork and dreams.

If Downstairs had two sides—two versions, or halves, or whatever—then Niko had passed into the other one the night of the party, through the unlocked fridge. The Niko I saw stumbling out of the hall that night, sick and wanting sleep, was the wrong Niko. A different Niko. The one my Niko had passed in the hall.

And that Niko didn't quite fit in. Everything was a little off about him, and from his perspective, I suppose, about me.

But that Niko had found two keys. We had no idea where he'd found them. But if he'd passed through the fridge with one of them—and here I will compress the part where we opened another bottle of vodka rather than accept the ridiculousness of this garbage fairy tale premise where a magical Frigidaire is a gateway between worlds, slept it off, suffered through ugly hangovers the next day, and reconvened late in the afternoon with some Aspirin—if the other Niko came through the fridge just before my Niko had, that could explain why my Niko had found it unlocked and open, was able to pass through.

And earlier—if we followed this chain of logic—I'd been drinking from a different vodka bottle, in a different house, with that other Niko. The one with the keys.

I'd stolen them and passed through to this side of Downstairs— the wrong side—and maybe some other me had been doing the same thing. I only avoided him by my sudden detour, when I sensed something wrong up ahead and ducked into the side room with the sheet-covered furniture, to let him pass by. And now we were both in the wrong house, on the opposite side from where we'd started.

"And both of them are on the wrong side, too," Niko said, still wincing from the hangover.

I licked my lips, head also still spinning, wondering if it would be okay to take two more Aspirin. Or four more. "But these other two, if they exist." I still couldn't quite surrender to this madness. "They could come back any time they wanted, right? And so could we."

"Because the key's still in the lock on their side." Niko frowned. "And you've got the one for this side. Both keys are back where they should be now. One for us and one for them."

"Unless there are two keys for this side too."

"No. You said the first one you tried didn't work, even though it looked the same? I think there's exactly two keys. One for each side. The other me ended up with both, somehow. I guess if he found one and went through, he'd know right where to look for the second."

We stared at each other.

"What does that mean?" I asked.

"I have no fucking idea. But shit, man, I'm glad you're here." He ran a hand through his curls, face pale. "I seriously wasn't handling this on my own. This whole last week, things weren't right. *You* weren't right, and I couldn't stand that, man. I was going crazy without you. Doubting everything, you know how I get. Doubting who I even was. But this, this is..." He waved his hand back and forth between the two of us, then knocked it on the table. "You get me. We're tight. Yeah? In it together, I mean. It's good. I'm glad."

I didn't say anything, but I didn't have to. I felt the same way and he knew it.

I slept in his room that night, in a sleeping bag beside his bed. He didn't want to be alone. I'd kind of wanted some time to process everything but I didn't protest too much. I liked being his anchor. He kept us both up late talking about random bullshit, rambling. It was okay. Everything was upside down. Old comforts couldn't hurt.

We slept in the next day. Call me a coward, but buried in my sleeping bag I could pretend I wasn't in the wrong universe.

Things were definitely wrong. Now that I was looking, I couldn't deny it. Familiar people acted strange in a way you couldn't put your finger on. Colors seemed indefinably different shades. A vague sense of off-ness suffused everything, like a movie with the sound a frame out of sync.

After looking more closely, things were off about my room. There was an unfamiliar dress shirt on a hanger. My copy of Samuel Delany's *Dhalgren* was missing, along with all the other books of his I'd discovered after reading that one. It wasn't quite my room, I realized. It was someone else's.

It was mostly little things, so we grasped at each quantitative difference, each change we could pin down. One night one of our housemates kept saying something I didn't understand. She was going on about getting a parking ticket and kept saying it was the "fourth fucking time" it had happened.

"What's that word you're saying?"

"Fucking," she clarified, unhelpfully.

"No," I said. "Count up in ordinals. You know first, second..."

She blinked at me. "First, second, third, fourth, fifth."

Fourth. Instead of fourd.

Things were different here.

We didn't find too many obvious changes. My favorite Disney movie, *The Golden Bird*, seemed never to have existed here, replaced by something called *The Aristocats*. Postage stamps cost 35 cents instead of 33. Usually we weren't quite sure whether something had actually changed, or we were losing our goddamn minds.

We danced around it for a while, but finally the phrase came out: parallel universes. But it didn't really satisfy. Why these two universes in particular, out of a supposedly infinite number? Why were they connected via a series of poorly decorated basement rooms and linked together by a refrigerator, of all things?

At one point, feeling overwhelmed, I called home—not to tell mom what was happening because I didn't want her to freak, just to hear her voice—but the answering machine said they were on vacation till the end of the month. This was annoying both because I hadn't heard about any long vacation, and because "we" presumably meant her and my sister, and for some reason I hadn't been invited, which made me feel even more out of place and abandoned. I was three hours away, not on a different planet.

Feeling rejected, I went record shopping, adding a couple hundred dollars to my already terrifying credit card debt in exchange for a small stack of LPs. Lately I'd gotten obsessed with sci-fi audio book recordings. I found a few treasures at my usual haunts: Leonard Nimoy reading Ray Bradbury, and a six-record set of one of the Dune novels, read by Frank Herbert himself, still shrink-wrapped. More and more I only bought stuff in its original wrapping, unopened, sleeves protected from scuffs and wear marks, the records inside unplayed and undamaged, which is how I'd keep them.

Bradley had been the one who got me into records. I was a cassette tape kid and a Discman high schooler, but he'd hooked me on the sound of LPs, the joys of flipping through those big bold album covers in record stores; of lying on your back blissing out to the singular magic of some rare recording or old favorite spun roaring back to life, twenty-two minutes at a time.

After what happened in the cafeteria I didn't talk to him for a long time. He kept trying to see me. Calling the house, throwing pebbles at my window late at night. I ignored it all. I was so angry at him, for taking something from me I couldn't quite encircle or define: more than my coming out, but all the changes inside me that would have led up to it, too. For putting me in danger, and my friends, my family.

He didn't give up. He left long, rambling messages on our answering machine, slipped love letters under the door. He was waiting outside the house one day when I walked home from my new school and there on the front porch, wearing our backpacks, I told him I didn't want to see him any more and broke his heart.

He begged me. He pleaded. He screamed and then apologized for screaming; he groveled, he cried. He told me he couldn't live without me. He said I'd never find anyone who'd love me like he did. He said if I threw away what we had because of the bigots and bullies I'd be letting them win.

When my little sister got home he started begging and pleading with her to talk some sense into me, and when he grabbed her arm and started shouting at her too, that's when I hit him.

He kept calling and writing and dropping by the house until my mom got the police involved. After that I never saw him again.

Probably it was because of what happened with Bradley that

I got so guarded with my friendships later on. I kept a polite distance from most people, and almost everyone I met in college stayed an acquaintance, not a friend. It was as if I'd lost the knack of getting close to people, of letting them in. Connecting. Niko broke through that, somehow, became the first close friend I'd had in years, and even though I tried not to cling too hard, eventually I figured out why it had been so difficult not to. He'd been clinging back.

We stayed close, maybe inevitably now that we were the only matching pair in this entire universe. It felt easy to be closer to him, for us both to need each other. It felt right. A relief from the wrongness all around us.

He thought my airlock idea had legs. Downstairs was made from house-stuff: hallways and empty rooms and appliances. A fridge was one of the few devices in that context that could maintain a seal. It was a cute concept except it didn't actually explain anything.

It took a long time to convince him we needed to go back down.

"Maybe we can just stay here, and they can stay there," he said. "So everything's off a little. So what? It felt way more wrong to get close to..." He waved a hand. "Him. Whoever. My handsome twin. So maybe we should leave well enough alone. Brick the fucker up and never look back."

Then the headaches started.

They were odd headaches. Not severe. A tinge of nausea and dizziness, like stepping off one of those fairground rides that whirls you around, and only a very distant pain. They came and went. But I took them as an ominous sign.

Niko said he'd been getting them all week. Oh. And they'd been getting stronger.

So the headaches more than anything convinced us. We had to go back down, try to get back through. Or maybe there were other points of connection. We'd barely started exploring. There was so much left.

But first we had to solve what Niko called the Mere Paradox. He threw a spoon at me when I said this back to him.

"No, smart-ass. A *Mirror* Paradox. We're obviously in this creepy weird sync with them." We were in his room with the door shut, and he was pacing the two-and-a-half steps of cleared floor while I lay on his bed, thinking. "Example. Me and the other Niko both went exploring on the same night. The other side, the other house, they were having a party that night too. We both saw that. The decor, uh, such as it was, was the same on both sides, or close enough. He and I were so synced up that we got to the fridge only minutes apart. He beat me, so he came through first, and then we passed in the hall." He stopped pacing, shuddered, and drummed his fingers on a bulky MIDI keyboard propped up against a wall gathering dust. "Two. A week later, both pairs of us end up getting drunk off vodka on the same night. Oh, there's these little differences—one side finishes the bottle, the other doesn't, and this me didn't get a certain text message that night—but both versions of you decide to go exploring. Again, you get to the pool room only minutes apart. For the most part it's like we're staying in a kind of lockstep, despite the superficial differences."

"Your conclusion, professor."

"If we go down to explore, they will too. We meet in the middle, and bam." He shook his head. "Exactly what we don't want to happen." He saw I was still confused, so he scribbled two arrows on his whiteboard, pointed right at each other. "The fridge is the connection point. The only way each pair of us can get back, so far as we know. But if we go back there, so will they. It's like we're trapped on two sides of a mirror. We each want to touch it, but we can't do it at the same time."

"Would it really be so bad?"

He glared down at me. "You don't trust that feeling? I got a lot closer than you, and man, it was the worst. I don't know what was causing it or why, but every part of my body was screaming something was wrong, was sick, was going to harm me." He sighed and flopped down next to me. "So if we can't get close to each other, but trying to cross through will bring us together, then what do we do?"

"Okay, so we explore at random." I sat up. "Every branch, we roll dice. Even if the others are in sync and pick the same time to explore, they'll go down different paths."

He shook his head. "I think the lockstep runs deeper than that. Even randomness could be part of it. The coffee stain. Remember? We both passed the one on this side, coming out. That's what made you assume you were in the same place. Because it was identical, right? If both versions of me spilled coffee and both made exactly the same stain, I bet dice would fall the same way too."

"How do we know it's identical? Did you really stop and look that close?"

That got him. Niko would jump off a bridge to win an argument. A few minutes later we were headed back down the stairs, keeping up a forced light banter. It helped that the coffee stain was close to the surface, and far enough away from the fridge that even if the others went down at the same time, to look at their stain, we'd be nowhere near each other.

No one had cleaned up after the party—in fact, the other housemates had stopped coming down here at all, inexplicably— so there were still Christmas lights and red plastic cups strewn around the big room. Weirdly comforting. We retraced our first trip through the upper hallways to the coffee stain, and got down on hands and knees to study it. I immediately felt foolish.

"This won't prove anything. We never looked at the original this close." I shrugged. "I don't know. It looks the same to me."

"But exactly the same?" Niko bent closer, excited. "No, I don't think so. I don't remember this trail of droplets off to the side here. Do you?"

We argued about it for a few minutes, but it was like grabbing soap in a bathtub. I'd read enough textbooks about memory and perception to know neither of us could accurately recall specifics of the other stain—it was weeks since we'd seen it and the details hadn't seemed important at the time.

I got up, shaking my head. "What is this even meant to prove? Does it matter if they're identical or not?"

"It matters," he said emphatically, "because if it's exactly the same then the two sides are in total lockstep. We can't do anything different from them and they can't do anything different from us. But if the stains are different—even just a little—then there's a chance to break out of the pattern. Do something unique. That could be huge."

"But we know we're not exactly in sync," I said. "For one thing, they somehow found keys down here. We never did that. They know things we don't, which means they're factoring that knowledge into their plans right now."

"Like where they found them in the first place," he said, rubbing his temples. "Right."

We sat in the hall for a minute in glum silence. I stared at the coffee stain, like it was an inkblot that would resolve into something sensible if I could make my mind work the right way.

"There's other differences," I said. "When I went down, I felt like something was wrong, and I went and hid like a baby. The other version of me didn't do that. We did different things."

"Yeah," he said, closing his eyes. "I'm actually worried about that."

"You were just saying you wanted us to be unique."

He rubbed his forehead. Maybe he was getting another headache. "The two sides are nearly identical, as far as we can tell. The two versions of us are nearly identical too. So far, at least. But I don't know. Maybe if we start acting different, if we diverge too far..."

"What?"

He shrugged. "Don't know. Just a thought. Probably garbage, never mind."

I closed my eyes and leaned my head back against the wall. "I'm late for work."

"Gotta make rent," he muttered. "Wouldn't want to get evicted now."

Niko was scared. He stayed close to me almost all the time, hanging out in my room, by the TV, wherever I was. This was a familiar pattern, actually: whenever he got overwhelmed he made me his full-time validator, babbling his interior monologue, running every decision big and small by me, ending most sentences with "Right?" or "Yeah?" It was like outsourcing his ego. I let him do it, like I always did. But I felt guilty, too, because it couldn't be healthy.

We kept talking, and our half-assed theories began to crystallize into a plan.

We rounded up a bunch of dice, some tarot and playing cards, loose change, a dreidel, and a stack of books, and devised a procedure—a ridiculously complicated procedure lasting almost an hour—to end up with two numbers, after several dozen iterations: the first between one and twenty-four, and the second between one and sixty. An hour, and a minute. The theory was that even if both sides were so close even randomness tended to turn out the same, if we stacked that randomness on top of itself, compounding chance on chance, it might be a wedge to split that sameness apart. Niko showed me a tiny video on his computer about strange attractors, said this was chaos theory in action, the butterfly effect. Whatever. We were making wild guesses.

But the hope was that even if the other versions of us were doing the exact same thing—following an identical procedure—their numbers would drift apart and they'd end up generating a completely different time.

Which would allow each pair of us to pass through without

crossing paths.

So we had a plan. We just needed a time.

"In hindsight," Niko said, throwing back the last of the coffee and smacking his lips, "maybe we should have put a range on the fucking numbers. Dear god. I have to be at work in five hours."

It was just after three in the morning, and we were prepping to go down. The time we'd generated was 3:41. We hoped for their sake the guys on the other side got something more reasonable.

Niko was in a rough mood, and it wasn't just the time of day. His old jock friends had been ragging him about not hanging out. ("I have to pretend sports bloopers are funny, Ry. It's horrible.") Later he'd gotten a call from one or both of his parents about how his degree was progressing, which had not gone well. He spent the rest of the day in his room with the door shut blaring loud music and, apparently, watching a *Friends* marathon. Every time I listened at his door I kept hearing Joey say "How *you* doin'?" Laugh track. Maybe he was just watching the same episode on repeat. Late that night I knocked again and reminded him we had a three a.m. date. A long and mournful stream of cuss words came muffled through the door. After an ominous silence he opened it, looking bleak. "Whose stupid idea was this again?" he asked, then grimly set his alarm.

We'd planned a quick trip in and out, to minimize the chance of overlapping times. Once we passed through and got back up to the surface, our surface, we'd leave the house and stay away until the next day. The campus library stayed open all night and if you had a book in your lap they wouldn't usually hassle you for sleeping. The next morning, we'd come back home, the headaches would be gone, and everything would be back to normal. It made sense, except we were making it all up and had no idea if any of this would work or if we were playing make-believe.

Swinging up the bed did feel ominous now, though. I noticed for the first time that it creaked. Stupid. We were girded up with supplies even though it was supposed to be a quick trip—three flashlights each, water bottles, even granola bars. Niko had a pad of yellow sticky notes and flipped the edges of it compulsively, nervous: "in case we need to mark our way," he explained.

We'd never seen anything dangerous down there, exactly. We just knew something wasn't right, now. That it wasn't just a basement down there.

We knew. We knew nothing. The truth is that despite our attempts to rationalize, to explain, we were blind. Shooting in the dark. Grasping at straws from sci-fi movies and bad dreams.

We had no idea what was happening to us.

We headed down, quietly so as not to wake our housemates. Once we got Downstairs, we followed the well-beaten path toward the room with the pool and the fridge. Niko was jumpy, especially when we got to the first staircase into the dark zone. Every shadow seemed ominous and he muttered suspicions at everything. "I think this door moved," or, "Someone's been here, I can feel it." I tried my best to keep things light, to reassure him. He started idly doodling flip-book animations of a gruesome hanging on the pad of sticky notes.

On our way down the twisting stairs to the octagon room, he stopped at one landing and glanced down the hall branching off from it. With a choke, he stiffened and leapt back, gripping the flashlight like a sword.

"Jesus fucking Christ," he hissed. "What the shit is that?"

I looked.

Way down the hallway, past the reach of the flashlight, were two tiny glints, hovering maybe four feet off the ground, deep in the darkness.

My heart rate was through the roof and I couldn't breathe, but I raised my flashlight too, shined it down the hall. It revealed nothing but the glints. I felt paralyzed. But I saw how scared Niko was. How close both of us were to panic.

I gave him a mock salute. "Later, skater," I said, and started down the hall.

"The fuck are you doing?" Niko hissed from behind me. But I kept moving. I kept walking forward, eyes fixed on the glints, willing my light to get stronger, willing those eyes to resolve into something explainable, something benign.

"Shit," Niko said, and followed me. "Shit shit shit."

It only took a few more steps before we realized our mistake.

The hall ended in a T-junction. About four feet off the floor was one of those fake candelabra. The glints had been our flashlights, reflecting off its dull metal sheen.

I laughed; it was easy with all the relief flooding through me. "See? There's enough weird shit going on without jumping at shadows."

Niko forced a laugh out too, but his face was still pale and tense. "How could you tell? From back there?"

I shrugged. "I couldn't. This was the quickest way to find out."

"Great. My hero. Glad you weren't mauled by a shadowbear." But he was smiling now for real, and looking at me with respect.

He was right. That was stupid. Bravado is exactly the wrong response to what's happening.

"Let's hurry and get this over with." We walked back to the landing. Niko wrote "NOT THIS WAY" on a sticky note and slapped it on the wall, drawing an arrow down the hall. I added a smiley face; he grabbed the pen back and drew some demon eyebrows on it.

We made it the rest of the way to the pool room without incident, and climbed the ladder. I was on edge, waiting for any signs of that sick feeling of wrongness, but nothing happened, and there were no creepy doppelgängers waiting for us above the lip of the pool.

"Okay," Niko said, clapping his hands: he was spooked too, I could tell. "Let's do this. You want to do the honors?"

I pulled out the bent key and slipped it into the lock, turned it. It rotated with a smooth snick. I pulled the handle, and as I tugged the fridge door open past the familiar suction, the light inside came on.

Niko let out a strangled gasp and bent down, staring inside the door in horror. I stood frozen, still gripping the handle, unable to process what my eyes were telling me.

Because inside was no longer a vinyl-padded room and the inside of another door. Instead, we were staring down a smooth, white, rectangular tunnel, that went on and on as far as we could see.

≫ 6 ≪

"What the fuck is this?" Niko hissed. I didn't have an answer. We stared into the bright white hallway like it was a road to heaven, or to hell.

The first few feet were the same as when we'd passed through before, the same as the interior of any ordinary fridge. Vinyl walls, plastic crisper drawers below the clear floor, a tiny bright bulb in the ceiling. But it didn't end. It kept going. Every few feet another little white bulb above; vinyl walls extending farther and farther; and an endless highway of clear plastic shelf for a floor, eight inches above the vinyl floor. The lines extended to a perfect vanishing point, and for as far as we could see, nothing changed.

For the next few hours, we did our best to interrogate this new unwanted truth, but gained no new understanding, came no closer to reconciling it with our plans to go back through. First we threw some wadded-up sticky notes and granola bars down the tunnel. When nothing happened to them, we ventured inside. Walking was hard: the ceiling was too low to stand up straight, so you had to move forward in an awkward shuffle. We only made it a hundred feet in before we had to turn back: Niko had been looking over his shoulder every few seconds to make sure the door back out hadn't vanished while we'd turned our backs on it, and eventually bumped his head one too many times on the ceiling and had a full-on claustrophobic panic attack. We retreated, hearts racing and muscles cramping. The next hundred feet had looked just as identical, anyway.

We tried locking the fridge and unlocking it again, turning the key and opening the door a dozen different ways, like it was a car with an unreliable starter you needed the right knack to handle. The door always opened on that same impossible tunnel. We tried shouting down the tunnel, or staying quiet and listening, but our voices were swallowed up and the silence stayed relentless, unbroken except for the quiet hums of the row of tiny lights. Later we got braver, tried more drastic measures: Niko had a pocketknife and we took it to the tunnel walls. Underneath the vinyl was more vinyl. We gouged out a chunk eight inches deep before giving up. The floor felt like flimsy plastic, bending a little with our weight, but no amount of vigorous stomping shattered or even cracked it.

"We could get a bunch of food, mount an expedition," I suggested, half-heartedly. *It can't go on forever,* I wanted to say, but couldn't bring myself to. He didn't answer.

Finally, we gave up.

We climbed back down the ladder to the empty pool and stepped back into the hall. I was trying to think of next steps, more plans, but my body and mind were exhausted. I turned to pull the pool door shut behind us.

As I did I noticed a small yellow square was stuck to it.

"Niko," I gasped, breath failing me, "oh *shit*. There's a note. Someone left a note."

We stared at it, afraid to touch it. We saw immediately that it was the one we'd left earlier, at the junction with the glints. "NOT THIS WAY," it said in Niko's handwriting. But the smiley face with the demon eyebrows looked sinister now, malevolent.

The arrow pointed toward the pool room, and the fridge.

"It's them," Niko breathed, sagging back against the opposite wall, as far away from the note as possible. "Our doubles. They moved it. My god, Ry. They came here and moved it. They were right outside."

My mind whirled. "Then that means there must be another way through. Some way for them to get here."

"Maybe." He swallowed, face pale. "Or maybe there's something else going on. Something's down here with us, man. Fucking with us."

We stared at the note.

NOT THIS WAY.

The silence was almost painful.

Abruptly Niko turned and started back down the hall, toward the surface, not talking, not looking back. I was right behind him.

When I was a kid I got way into swimming one year, another obsession. I started going to the rec center pool every day after school, having mom drop me off there on weekends. They had a swim program and I shot through all the rankings. Minnow, Fish, Flying Fish, Salmon, Shark, Tiger Shark. I swam. I don't recall especially enjoying it: it was just something I did, like a job. Then at school one day someone asked me why I was so into it and I couldn't tell them. I could hold my breath for forever, which helped, but hardly seemed like a good reason. The truth was I had no idea why I was doing it, and that terrified me. What had made me start? I couldn't remember. I felt almost violated, possessed, like some outside force had tricked me into driving all my thoughts and energies into moving back and forth through lanes of water, over and over again, for months on end. I stopped not long after, in part because I was hitting puberty and changing clothes in front of other guys was becoming more and more mortifying, but I think really it was because I couldn't explain that compulsion and it scared me.

I felt it again, now. I wanted to stay Downstairs. Sure, I could rationalize this away: the only way back home was down here. But the real reason was that I wanted to find out what was down there, more than anything. I was driven to. Something was driving me. At least that's how it felt.

I didn't mention any of this to Niko. I knew if I did it might put him off exploring altogether.

We didn't say anything to each other on the way back, and when we climbed up through my bed and shut it, we split up. Niko went out the front door, I assumed to take a walk, without a word. I lay on my bed listening to records until I got too creeped out imagining what might be underneath me, and went out to curl up on the porch swing, instead.

The summer air was hot, with only the hint of a breeze, but felt infinitely better than the cold dead air down there.

I tried to think of anything else, but something kept dragging my brain Downstairs, as if it was too heavy to stay on the surface with me. No matter how often I clawed my way onto other topics, Downstairs and all the things we didn't know about it dominated my thoughts.

I had no idea what we should do next.

When Niko came back it was with a brown bag from the liquor store, and he went straight up to his room, not even looking at me. I didn't feel like talking to him either.

We didn't know what was going on; we didn't know how to stop it. We didn't know anything.

We might have stayed in our funk for another couple days, except something happened the next morning.

The local history lady had left me a voicemail at around 7:15, a solid fantasy movie and credits before I normally woke up. She'd been useless when I'd stopped by before, and her tone of voice in the message—"something a bit exciting's come to light about your house"—made me assume she'd dredged up some trivia as a pretense to get me to come back and keep her company. Maybe get me to join the local history society myself. A warm-blooded young person like myself could even aspire to become treasurer.

So it was a couple hours before I got around to calling her

back and asking when would be a good time to come over.

"Oh, come right away," she said, voice syrupy. "This really can't wait. Just wait till you see what I've found."

Not at all encouraged, I agreed to head over, and biked the mile or so to her fastidiously tidy house. The visit got off to an ugly start when she asked why I hadn't brought my colored friend this time. "Actually, he's Greek," I said through clenched teeth, and then wished I had the guts to say something else. She served me tea again, weak to the point of tastelessness, and spent so much time making small talk I'd convinced myself she hadn't found anything and this whole exercise was a waste of time. Worse, she kept glancing at my pride bracelet and pursing her lips, and then pretending not to have done either. I wanted to get out of there but was too mentally exhausted to remember how social interactions were supposed to work, what niceties would bring a conversation to an end.

The third or fourd time I pressed her about what she'd found, she got up with a triumphant smile and bustled out, returning a minute later with a file folder holding a few photocopies.

"I did some digging on your address," she said, "and found something rather interesting." She turned the last two words into an annoying sing-song. *Raaaaather intressting.* Trying to tune her out, I opened the file and pulled out the first page.

Clutching the page, I scanned the smudged text. It was a blurry copy of an old newspaper ad, maybe from around the turn of the century. It advertised, in a hand-drawn, swirling font, some attraction called "THE VORTEX."

I noticed the address and almost choked on my tea.

The ad looked for all the world like one of those terrible roadside attractions desperate for tourist dollars. MADAME ZOLA WILL READ YOUR FORTUNE, MEET BOBO THE CHUCKLING CLOWN, that kind of thing. IF YOU ONLY KNEW WHAT AWAITS YOU.

Towards the bottom, though, an image caught my eye. It was a drawing of two identical women with wavy, crimped hair and a distant expression, sad and remote. Actually, it looked like the same drawing printed twice, side by side. Both women stared vaguely down and to the left. THE SISTERS, said a caption above them, and then, below and smaller, the word DESCEND.

Running through the ad was something like a ribbon that, on peering closer, seemed meant to be a stylized stream of water. This was confirmed by a rhyme running alongside one part of it, in tiny, florid print:

> *A looking-glass held above this stream*
> *Will show your troubles like a dream*

There was no further explanation. Admission to the Vortex was ten cents and it was closed Sundays.

DESCEND.

I flipped to the other few pages in the folder as the woman twittered on about her sleuthing skills in the county archives. The second page was a short newspaper clipping about the Vortex being shut down—not over a grisly murder or string of disappearances but, of all things, a zoning controversy. A new mayor had instigated a crackdown on businesses operating improperly out of residential districts. There was no date but "1934" had been scrawled in pencil on the photocopy.

The final page was at first a mystery, an article—maybe even older than the Vortex ad—about an old Army post being torn down to make way for new housing. I pieced together from a few contextual clues ("the new university", "on top of the hill") that this was my neighborhood, and felt a sinking hunch our house was on the site of the old post.

The article recounted in brief the fort's unstoried history, built on the site of a spring which "bubbled up from a natural cavern" bricked up when the place was constructed. Nothing much of note had ever happened there. Built to keep white settlers safe from the natives they were busy exterminating, the post had never been attacked or even threatened.

"Once the fort was built and the spring bricked up, the Indians never again came near the place," the old article said by way of explanation.

She must have caught me staring at this sentence, because she leaned over and tapped it with a pencil. "Haunted." Her grin was smug.

"Excuse me?"

"Been seeing spirits, have you?" she asked. "Must be an old burial ground. Read a book about it once. When they're disturbed, young man, the ghosts of redskins get *very* angry."

I looked up at her with a flash of anger. "I think we say Native Americans now. And there's no ghosts. That's not it." I didn't know how, but I'd never been more sure of anything.

She puckered her mouth, glanced again at my pride bracelet. "Well. Should have realized you'd be the *sensitive* type."

I couldn't take this any more. Her racist bullshit aside, the notion that what was happening to me was a cute mystery for her to solve was so disconnected from the growing existential dread of the past few days I wanted to slap her. She was everyone who thought my problems had simple explanations, everyone who thought casting victims as villains made for good stories. For a moment, brief and burning, I hated her.

And that's when her face came unstuck.

This was back when movies were still celluloid, and at the second-run theater by our house the film would sometimes jump the gate, get misaligned. When that happened the image would smear, frames no longer projected neat one after the other but running liquid through the machine, all movement turned into vertical bands of distorted color; and the audio would go juddery, vague, and distant, recognizable but distorted. Clipped and monstrous.

This was like that but in three dimensions.

The woman exploded. Her face twisted and smeared, exposing blood and bone. The back of her tongue flapped against her pulsing epiglottis, her eyes round spheres peeling back, turning inside out, her lips deformed and pulled like taffy into a twisting shape that reached from the ceiling to her knees. Her fingers had gone long as tree branches and skinny like pencils, twisting and jerking backward at frantic angles; the pattern of her dress had multiplied and filled the empty spaces in the air and was so thick now I choked on it. Everything moved, everything in her sounded, and the sound was a scream, like her lungs were jet engines, her voice box a bleating thing the size of a cow being flayed alive.

I dropped the teacup and the files: I vaguely remember them tumbling toward the floor in slow motion, spilling and twisting around each other. I was screaming too. All I wanted was to get away. I stumbled back and my head cracked against a cabinet of china plates; I held up my hands to shield myself, as if such a pathetic act could matter against a thing so huge and horrible. It came toward me, moving fast. I couldn't stop it. My sanity frayed.

And then she snapped back into herself, and her voice returned to normal. Almost. It still juddered, like the floor beneath her vibrated a hundred times a second. And her skin was boiling and rippling, like something inside it was desperate to get out. Thousands of tiny somethings pushing and pounding with disproportionate strength against her wrinkled flesh.

She reached toward me—and maybe this was all in my head, maybe she was trying to help, reacting in shock to my reaction, what must have seemed like some kind of seizure—but as she opened her mouth to speak, the rippling distortions made it into a grin. A huge, horrible, ravenous grin, malevolent. Gleeful.

Her reaching fingers writhed, and her eyes were wide and round as saucers.

I jerked to my feet and ran.

For a while I didn't even know what direction I was running.

I bolted straight through intersections and past oblivious pedestrians, not seeing them. I wasn't thinking about anything at all. I didn't stop until a knife in my side brought me up short, bent me double, and I realized I'd been running a long time.

I collapsed on a patch of hot grass and threw up, retching and gasping. Gnats scribbled the air around me. Somewhere a dog barked.

I stayed there five or ten minutes, breathing jagged, looking down, studying my hands on the grass and my puke, dealing with those three things, the hands and the grass and the puke, not wanting or able to look up or deal with anything else. Nothing happened. After a while that started to help.

Eventually I climbed to my feet, got my bearings. I realized I knew where I was. I walked slowly back to our house.

I never went back for my bike.

When I got home, Niko was gone. I let myself into his bedroom and curled up on his bed, because I needed to be surrounded by something familiar. The smell of him was an anchor to reality. Maybe the only one.

I came in here sometimes when he was gone, usually only when he left the door unlocked. I didn't touch anything. I just wanted to see the pieces of his life in isolation from his too-bright self, read the story they told about him with no silhouette from that burning corona. Once I'd seen a brochure from the campus LGBT center in his trash can, and wondered about that for a long time: why he'd taken it, why he'd thrown it away.

I must have drifted off, because moments later the afternoon light was dying and his hand was on my shoulder, shaking it. I jerked awake, guilty excuses on my lips before I realized he didn't seem concerned about me breaking in. His hair was matted and he had a distant expression, staring past me.

"I took a piss," he said quietly, as if to someone standing behind my left shoulder, "and the bubbles were like eyes. There were thousands of them, floating. Staring. Iridescent, like oil. Something grinning underneath them, though, behind them. Something babbling and grinning and hungry and even when I closed the lid and flushed them away I could still hear them, down there, all of them..."

I sat up, grabbed his shoulders and shook him, then did it again, hard. His head flopped back and he grabbed my wrist, a faint annoyance reaching his face. I was glad to see anything there at all.

I let him focus on me before saying, "There's no eyes."

He stared at me.

I shook my head, more sure of it now. "It's not ghosts, or a thing out there, stalking us. It *is* us. We're what's wrong here. We're the ones who don't belong." I swallowed, bile still souring the back of my throat. "We're slipping. Losing our grip on... something. This whole world, maybe. Or it's losing its grip on us."

I had his full attention now.

"And I don't know what happens when we let go, or it does," I finished. "But I don't think it's good."

He stared at me, hopeless. "There's no way back."

"There is. There has to be." I took a breath. "We just have to find it."

≋ 7 ≋

We taped big sheets of artist's paper to the wall of his bedroom
to make a map, shoving piles of CDs and unwashed dishes and
dirty underwear and two scuffed snowboards out of the way to
make room. He transferred our notebook sketches to the wall
and we tried to fill in the rest from memory. It was imperfect,
because stairs down there ran up and down and the wall was
flat, and also because the hallways twisted at weird angles and
we didn't have surveying equipment to sort them out. But it was
a start.

It was also painfully incomplete. Dozens of doors had never
been opened, countless halls had only been glanced into. Almost
everything we had seen was from that single hall off the big
room, the one we'd tried on a whim our first time down. Other
than peering around the first couple corners, we hadn't explored
the other four halls at all.

Niko swept a hand across all the empty space. "We're fucked."

"Look," I countered, "we know the other versions of us found
a key, somewhere. And we also know the two sides are staying
almost exactly in sync. Close enough to spill coffee the same
way."

"Not close enough to leave each others' fucking sticky notes
alone."

"Still," I pressed on, "that means the keys can't have been too
well-hidden. We could have almost found one, walked right past

it. Maybe the only difference was a momentary decision about which door to go through, what wall to glance at."

"Doesn't matter." He stirred his coffee, morose, and sat it down to cool on his dresser, next to a half-empty older mug growing a skim of mold. "The keys are useless now, anyway."

"If there's one set of keys, there might be more. Other keys, other doors. And besides, we have no idea what else might be down there. We need to keep looking."

He ran a hand through his hair, a familiar gesture, but he looked changed. His eyes were getting sunken, from lack of sleep or some more worrisome deficiency. His face, so often laughing, hadn't smiled in days.

"Synchronicity," he said. "That's the problem."

"How do you mean?"

"I think we're getting out of sync with them. Day by day, decision by decision, we're losing our lockstep. And the more out of sync we drift, the harder it gets to go back."

"Speculation," I said, tired.

"And the deeper," he pressed on, "the deeper we'll have to go to find another way through."

"Bullshit." But I didn't have energy to argue with him. Clearly we couldn't solve anything from up here. We needed to go back down. We had to fill in the blank spaces on that map.

Our first Expedition departed the next morning. With a capital E, Niko said, to show we were taking this shit seriously now. We had backpacks, trail mix and energy bars, lots of flashlights and batteries, twine, spray paint, a compass, graph paper, whistles, and rope. Despite everything, I think the prep got us fired up a bit. If answers were down there, we'd find them. We skipped class and I called in sick to work, and we both agreed if necessary we'd do the same tomorrow, and the next day. Finding a way back was top priority.

We chose one of the unexplored halls off the big room, and decided to explore as much of it as we could, until we'd mapped it all or got too tired to keep going. We picked the one at the far end of the room, opposite the stairs back up. Right away we found something different.

The first few twists and turns were the familiar terrain we'd come to expect: carpet, wall sconces, scuffed doors. But after a short and confusing snarl of hallways and tiny rooms, the floorplan opened up into an area with a slightly different style of sconces, and longer, straighter hallways.

Except some of them went straight down.

We stood at the lip of one of these pits and stared over the edge. It was like someone had taken a regular hallway and stood it on end. The brown carpet went right over the lip and continued straight down, passing sideways doors, sideways wall sconces. Maybe seventy or eighty feet down, it hit a carpeted bottom and leveled out again, branching in opposite horizontal directions. The pit filled the exact center of a junction; we could step around the corners into hallways leading off in the three other directions from the one we'd arrived. It was a five-way intersection, all at right-angles.

A couple dozen paces down one of those halls was another pit.

"What is this," Niko sighed, "challenge mode?"

When you think of treacherous terrain a basement hallway isn't the first thing that comes to mind, but clutching the corner and peering vertiginously down, the pit looked as unscalable as the Matterhorn. There was nothing to get a grip on, except the doorways every twenty feet or so. Clearly we couldn't get down without climbing gear, nor come back up without it either.

If you fell... if you got stuck down there...

We stepped carefully around the pit (which was awkward and terrifying because it came right up to the ninety-degree edge of the wall) and kept exploring on the same level. But the pits were everywhere. Each horizontal hall would dead end sooner or later, and the side rooms were all small and empty. Some of them had hallway pits, too, leading down from their exact center. After an hour we'd mapped out everything we could get to without a climbing harness. Other than going back to the big room, there was no way forward except fourteen pits, each at least fifty feet deep.

"Difficult could be good." Niko perked up. "This is the first thing we've had to work for. Maybe means there's something interesting down there."

"Or maybe one of the other hallways leads to a room filled floor to ceiling with keys. No point guessing."

We went back to explore one of the other halls—we didn't have much choice—and found something different there, too. All the doors on one side opened onto a vast dark room piled floor to ceiling with couches.

Niko leaned casually against the door and poked his head inside with a suave expression. "Hey," he called into the shadows, "How *you* doin'?"

The room began like all the others, although unlit: a regular door and the same style carpet. But we couldn't see a far wall, nor a wall to either side, maybe in part because the couches started a few feet in. There were a lot of them. Couches, chairs, recliners, loveseats, and sectionals, upholstered or varnished in a hundred styles, all dusty but ranging in condition from falling apart to so new they were still wrapped in plastic. They were mostly upright but some were wedged in at crazy angles, like movers had started systematically and then given up halfway through, throwing the rest on top in careless chaos.

But the arrangement was orderly enough that there were pathways through the furniture. Tunnels you could stoop-walk or crawl on all fours through. They branched and split constantly, a warren walled with sofas and lazy-boys and stools, a child's dream of a couch fort city brought to life. Our flashlights cast scattering shadows through the maze, but couldn't penetrate far.

"Promising," Niko said. "They're making us work for it."

"There's no 'they,'" I said automatically, mostly because I didn't want to think about it. "And it's the same problem again. We can't risk getting lost down here."

"But this is easier, man. We don't need specialized equipment. Just some way to leave a path. Hansel and Gretel, like you said."

Or maybe Ariadne. I had a ball of twine in my pack, so we settled for a simple solution: tying one end to my ankle, and the other around the doorknob. After some deliberation, we decided to keep our packs on, despite the awkwardness of crawling the maze with them. Having girded ourselves with stuff, we felt naked without it now.

We set off to map.

Crawling through the maze was surreal. The furniture painted by the bright of our headlamps made us feel foolish, like kids crawling around grandma's basement with the lights out. But the scale glimpsed in the shifting shadows, the distance traversed by our bodies and soon felt in our knees and ankles, spoke to confusing and frightening immensities, the deepness of caves, an underworld. The space went on and on. There was too much of it for reason, for safety, for sense.

We moved carefully at first, stopping to map each twist and turn, trying not to be unnerved by the way our lights carved a thousand sweeping shadow-shapes out of those tunnels of furnishings, moving and twisting like something alive. But as we started to realize the extent of the space, Niko developed a new strategy: push towards the center, or at least away from the long wall we'd entered from. Find the middle, if there was one. If it didn't go on forever.

What happened next caught us completely unprepared.

We'd started moving in a steady direction, as near as we could manage. I'd begun to feel almost cheerful: we were solving the mystery, peeling back this place's secrets. Surely it was just a matter of time before we found a way back home.

And then something *yanked* my ankle from behind.

I gasped and twisted around. The twine tied to my ankle was taut, and pulling me with terrible force, starting to drag me backwards. I cried out, digging my fingers into the carpet.

I collided with the padded side of a dusty couch and heard a clattering groan as furniture shifted all around me, pushed out of place. Weight shifted alarmingly above.

"What the fuck, *help me!*" I shouted. The loop around my ankle was viciously tight, cutting off circulation. My fingers scrabbled for purchase but the carpet wasn't shaggy enough to grip.

Niko scrambled back towards me, shrugging out of his pack and grabbing my arm. But as he pulled me back the twine dug into my ankle like a vise, like the pressure would saw the line straight through my foot. It *hurt.* I couldn't understand why it hadn't snapped. "Cut it, fucking cut it!" I gasped.

He cursed and let me go, whipping back around to zipper open his pack, letting the line start to drag me away. I reached out to grab a chair leg but only succeeded in dragging the whole thing along with me, screeches of metal-on-wood and the ominous clutter of shifting weights and balances sounding above and all around; and I let go before the whole nightmare could crash down around us, dividing us, burying us alive.

I panicked. My mind flashed through visions of monsters waiting at the edge of the maze, reeling me in, each sway of my headlamp birthing a new imagined terror out of the confusion of shapes around me. A horned demon. Some evil-eyed little girl from a shitty horror movie. And then the history lady flashed into my head, inside-out and distorted past the breaking point, eyes white and wide; and I started babbling

DESCEND

mind slipping towards the only place it might be safe

IF YOU ONLY KNEW WHAT AWAITS YOU

and Niko cut the twine.

I missed the lead-up in my nightmare, but he'd dug through

his pack for the Swiss army knife, lost at the bottom with the camping gear, then struggled to squeeze ahead of me without kicking me in the face or knocking anything down on top of us. He told me later he'd barely touched the blade to the twine when the taut line snapped, whipping away in a fraction of a second.

He had to spend a minute calming me down. My mind had skidded toward some rarely glimpsed drop-off, pulled edgeward by a dark and primal gravity, and it took time to climb handhold by handhold back up to the light.

What brought me back, prosaically enough, was the growing unpleasant tingling in my foot. Pins and needles: painful, but familiar. The knot on the twine had slipped down and pulled a tight loop around my leg just above the ankle, digging half an inch into my jeans. Niko helped me cut it off and I sat rubbing my foot for a long time, calming down, waiting.

Listening.

After maybe fifteen minutes we started back, Niko up front with the knife. I was equally terrified bringing up the rear, though, constantly looking over my shoulder, miserable and afraid. The furniture right around us had been dragged out of shape, the first few feet of couch fort distorted, unstable, but the rest of the way back was unchanged. We swung the lights back and forth ahead but could see nothing but a forest of shadows.

Maybe they really were alive.

After a few dozen feet we found the cut end of the twine, slack and unmoving. We followed it all the way back to where we'd come in.

It was no longer tied to the doorknob, like we'd left it. The twine lay coiled up in a neat loop. Right outside the threshold.

≫ 8 ≪

"So this is huge," Niko was saying. We were in the funny-shaped room behind the closet with the unfinished board game, dust gathering on unresolved plans for world domination. We'd moved all our expedition gear in here; we didn't want to explain things to anyone else, and the rest of the housemates had forgotten this room even existed. I rubbed the ugly bruise ringing my ankle, sitting on the grimy hardwood floor with my pant leg rolled up.

"Oh yeah?" I winced, prodding a tender spot.

"It's the first concrete sign there's something down there. Not glints of light. Not sounds. Something physical."

"Yeah, reassuring."

He conceded the point, slumping down next to me. "But why now? What brought this on? Is the maze forbidden? Did we violate some kind of policy?"

"Marking our way."

"What?"

"It's the first time we've tried to leave a permanent trail, something unambiguously marking the way back. Maybe whatever it is... ugh." It still felt awful to verbalize it, give it that kind of legitimacy. "Maybe it didn't appreciate that."

"What about the spilled coffee? That's a kind of a marker. We didn't get in trouble for that, and it didn't disappear or anything. Maybe whatever's down there doesn't want us exploring the furniture maze. Because it leads to something. Something big."

I punched the wall, suddenly angry. "Who knows? None of it makes any sense anyway."

"That'll go on our tombstones. A week from now, when we're dead of fucking dimension poisoning."

"Well hey, dude, it's either that or lung cancer thirty years from now." I mimed taking a drag off a smoke. "At least dimension poisoning's probably quicker."

He laughed despite himself, and I chalked up a mental win. Cheering him up, making him smile, was so ingrained in me I barely noticed I was doing it any more. Maybe that day, I shouldn't have been. It wasn't exactly a situation to be cheerful about.

Do I do it because I really want him to be happy? Or is it that I can't stand it when he's sad?

"I'm not going down there again," he said with grim finality.

We both contemplated that for a long minute.

"Okay fine, I am. You're right. You win. We find a way back. Somehow."

"There's monsters up here, too," I said softly.

He sniffed. "Or maybe we're the monsters, man. Crawled out from under the bed."

We decided to explore the vertical shafts, instead of going back into the maze. We didn't know whether what had happened was a message or a provocation. I thought the bruises on my ankle were message enough: Keep Out. Niko argued that was exactly why we should ignore it. Wherever they don't want you to go is probably the most interesting place to be. On the other hand, maybe the message had been like fences around Chernobyl.

Maybe whatever was farther in was worse.

So we settled on the shafts, which had the virtue of being unusual and promising terrain without even mild signs of demonic infestation. One of Niko's ex-hobbies was rock climbing, but he'd stopped after the accident jacked up his wrists. Bits of gear still lingered around his overstuffed bedroom, though, so we'd assembled some rope, harnesses, carabiners, and a couple of grappling hooks we found at the sporting goods store. The box called them "Grip Monkeys," which seemed incongruously cheerful.

We picked the first pit, since they all seemed about the same, and set about securing the grapples in a doorjamb in a way that would hold our weight. We'd each go down on our own rope, one at a time and using the second as backup. We also had extra Grip Monkeys in our pack, in case something happened to these.

Along with the usual gear, we also brought down a camcorder. We were too broke to afford the newer all-digital cameras, so we borrowed one that shot on Hi-8 tape. This was before the whole found footage craze, so we didn't think to take the camera down the pit with us and record weepy confessionals into it: we were going to leave it down the hall from the shaft, trained on the pit and our ropes and the Grip Monkeys, hopefully capturing anything that tried to mess with us.

When we were ready, and since we didn't have a tripod, I left the camera on the floor a dozen paces back, pointed at the pit, and hit record. We shouldered our packs and Niko tied on to the rope. Moving carefully, he stepped over the lip, and started to rappel down the carpeted "floor" of the shaft. I watched his grapple nervously, but it held his weight, tines set deep into the solid wood of the door frame.

The bottom of the shaft seemed a mile down with Niko dangling above it, but probably only dropped about seventy feet. He moved fast and soon was stepping onto the once-again-horizontal carpet at the bottom. He shined his light back up at me and gave the all-clear.

I followed him down, trying to think only in particulars about what was happening and not the terrifying big picture. I focused on old climbing lessons, what my hands were doing. One thing at a time. Presently I'd made it down too.

The hall at the bottom of the pit stretched off to either side, like we were at the junction of an upside-down T. Detaching from our dangling ropes, we picked a direction and began to explore.

Things got weird down there.

The hallways continued on as they had above, and there were more pits. But now they didn't go straight down. Not quite. They descended at angles ranging from severe to subtle, never quite true to vertical. Some were almost ramps. Others changed their angle or gradually twisted as they dropped. And while the pit we'd rappelled down was lit, none of these were. They plunged down into darkness.

There were more of them, too. A lot more. Dozens and dozens. Most opened from the middle of a hallway, filling its width: easy to jump across, but wearing a pack you felt clumsy, were acutely aware you were one stumble away from a very bad time.

We decided to avoid unnecessary leaps, but the pits were so thick they hedged us in, pushed us inexorably towards an unknown destination. If we tried to veer too far off course, they'd get denser, and we'd have to backtrack or turn aside, angling back to our former heading. And the longer we followed it, the more the hallway angles edged off true.

It was subtle at first. But the horizontal hallways became less and less level. We'd stumble on a floor that canted slightly left, or tilted a half-degree up or down. The walls, too, were growing angled, some leaning outward a degree or two instead of staying neatly parallel, or bent a little bit inward at mismatched angles. It made us feel drunk. You've seen so many well-constructed hallways in your life, your brain doesn't know how to process ones that don't behave.

We passed through one long hall that started leaning left and kept going as we moved down its length, twisting through a full three hundred and sixty degrees. I don't mean it was actually moving: imagine holding a long strip of paper, a hand gripping each end, and rotating one wrist to twist an end around. That was the shape the hallway made. The wall tilted and became the floor as we walked, and we tromped across closed doors, the rooms beneath them echoing. Then we were walking on the ceiling, stepping over light fixtures. By the time the hall ended it had rotated all the way around, and we were back on carpet again.

That wasn't the weird part.

The helix hall had opened into a grid of rooms with open doorways and no connecting corridors. After moving through these into an exit hallway, I called for a break. We hadn't been talking much, lost in our own thoughts. I said something about the weird hallway and Niko seemed confused.

"Weird how?"

"Twisting all the way around like that. You think it's significant?"

He didn't know what I was talking about.

I asked him to describe the path we'd taken to get here. Raising a skeptical eyebrow, he did. Everything was right except he called the part before the grid "a long, straight hallway."

"Nothing unusual about it?"

He blinked. "No, not that I saw. What are you getting at?"

"You don't remember, like, walking on the ceiling."

He frowned. "Are you fucking with me?"

I closed my eyes. I could remember the awkwardness of walking against that steepening angle, shifting a foot to shuffle awkward through the trough of an edge turned into two sloping floors. The way the sound had changed as the surface beneath our shoes went from carpet to drywall. The changing angle of the light as it hit us from below, from the side, from above.

I told him. When I'd finished, he looked sick, and angry.

"If you're messing with me, man..."

"I'm not. I swear. I'm not."

He hunched back into himself, looking despite his height like a tiny, cornered animal. Hunted.

"This changes things." His voice was small.

"How do you mean?"

He sniffed. "Alters the equation, you know. If you and I can't even see the same things any more... we're lost. In every sense that matters."

We vividly described our current surroundings to each other. Past things we'd seen: the octagon room, the pool.

Everything matched up.

It didn't make us feel any better.

"Maybe..." I grasped for something to say. Niko was scared now, I could tell, more scared than me. He needed me to calm him down. "Maybe I imagined it. You get that sense down here sometimes, right? Like thinking's almost enough to make it real?" He eyed me, uncertain. "Maybe I was daydreaming and got confused. We've been under a lot of pressure. I mean I don't know. A mistake."

He stared right through me. "You don't really believe that, do you?"

My face flushed. "I—"

"Don't just tell me what I want to hear, Ry. Don't ever do that. You got me? If I can't trust you..." He swallowed. My face flushed. The accusation stung.

"Let's go back," he said. "Let's go back and look, right now. Sort this out."

"No," I said at once, instantly terrified. I didn't want to know. Because no resolution to this was good. One of us couldn't trust our senses, or both of us couldn't. Or something was much more wrong than that.

Or, a voice whispered in my head, *maybe he's lying. Maybe he did see it, and he's just pretending he didn't.* I shook my head, but the voice persisted. *Who knows what else he's pretending about?*

Maybe he was thinking the same thing about me.

"We should go back," Niko said, miserable. "And if we don't both see the same thing in that hall, we need to abort. Get the fuck out of here, rethink this whole thing. This is *fucked up*, man. We're out of our depth. We're losing control."

"We can't quit now." I felt unaccountably calm. "If we let ourselves get spooked by every new thing that happens down here, we'll never figure out what we came down here to figure out. That's what we're looking for, right? The strange bits?" I gestured ahead. "We should see where this leads. Explore as far as we can before turning back. That was the plan, right?"

He stared yearningly back at the entrance to the grid of rooms, the path to the hallway that was or wasn't a helix. Then he turned his eyes to me. Resentful.

Suspicious.

"Yeah," he said. "It was."

Once at the peak of my swimming days I'd had a chance to swim in the ocean. It was a school trip and there was a beach day and some of the other guys were going to do it but the thought alone terrified me. Not because of waves or rip tides or sharks. In a pool, you know, through goggles, the universe becomes a smooth abstraction: white and well-lit concrete on all sides, contained, chemicals and filters flushing out anything but you. Sounds are muffled. Gravity's on break. There's no place for anything to hide, and even when you can't touch bottom, you know it's there, a few feet below.

The ocean is different in every conceivable way. Standing in the surf would be one thing, but swimming out past where my feet could touch the sand? The thought crushed me with primal terror, compressed me. An unknowable void stretching down beyond my flailing bare feet. What it might contain. Years later I tried reading Lovecraft and thought of that sensation again when he talked about cosmic horror, something so vast and inhuman it could shatter you, so close it could reach out and brush your toes. I couldn't make it through more than a couple stories. I couldn't shake that image.

I couldn't shake it now.

We kept going.

The halls branched and spread out endlessly. We gave up trying to map, other than the route back. We passed through regions of dark and regions of light. The decor rarely varied from its ubiquitous blandness. Sometimes little things were wrong. A door turned sideways, opening outward. A knob embedded in the ceiling, unable to be turned. Crown molding running in a line a foot above the carpet. We searched around these anomalies, but never found anything useful.

Some of the rooms got larger, too big for rooms in a house. More like a school gymnasium. Still the same carpet, though. And it felt like we were seeing more of the anomalies, the farther in and deeper down we got. An explosion of pipes and plumbing, sticking out of a wall for no particular reason; rooms that were two feet wide or with fifty-foot ceilings. It was like the deeper we went, the more flexible the rules became—of architecture, of stability, of god knows what else.

Behind one unassuming door we found something that looked almost like a backstage, with a wood floor painted black instead of a carpet, cinderblock walls with folding chairs stacked against them by the hundreds. But no curtain, no audience, no racks of lights above. In fact there was nothing above: the walls rose up beyond the range of our flashlights.

In the exact center of the room was one of those caged metal utility ladders, climbing up into that darkness.

"You see that, right?" Niko asked, wide-eyed. I did.

Mostly because it was going up and not down, we decided to try it. Or I decided, anyway, hands gripping the cool metal rungs before Niko could raise an objection. I felt reckless down here, brave enough to try anything. The exact opposite of the me on the surface.

Besides, the ladder looked just like the one at my junior high when I'd been on stage crew. I'd climbed it a million times. The metalwork of the cage felt like a blanket. Safe.

Within a minute I'd climbed disturbingly high. I didn't look down but the beam of Niko's flashlight, trained on me, had faded to glimmers, washed out by my own. Everything around and above was dark. And *quiet*. All Downstairs was quiet, of course, but here it seemed monstrously so, a quiet of infinitudes, even the sounds of my own body sucked away into the emptiness around me.

Niko seemed so far away.

"Find anything up there?" he asked, putting a hand on my shoulder. Startled, I looked down. My hands were still gripping the rungs of the ladder, but my foot was on the floor of the stage. I was on the ground. Niko was beside me.

"What happened?" I felt dizzy.

He frowned. "You climbed up for a while, then you came back down. Anything up there?"

I made him try. The same thing happened. I watched him climb up, high into the darkness above. Then, without missing a beat, he reversed course and came back down. When he made it back to me he was as startled as I'd been. He felt like he'd been climbing up the whole time.

We tried experiments. Keeping in verbal contact. Focusing on our movements. With enough of that, it was possible to realize that you'd started moving down again before you'd come all the way back. But always with a sick and juddering sense of grinding gears: one part of your brain kicking in and telling another it had been looking at things wrong. It took a moment to perceive, like an optical illusion. We stopped after a particularly nauseating moment when I was listening to Niko below me chanting *You're coming down, you're coming down, you're coming down*, and all my senses were telling me that was wrong, that I was still climbing up, climbing up, climbing up, and when the truth crashed into my perception I felt such a wave of sickness that I almost lost my grip on the ladder, had to clutch it shivering for minutes, cold sweat breaking out all over my body. After that we decided to stop experimenting.

We were getting tired. Just before turning back, though, we found one last curious room. We could hear it before we opened the door.

The room was the size of a squash court, though not quite as tall, the whole thing covered in green bathroom tile, even the inside of the door we came through. A sink rose serenely from its center. Scalding water blasted from the faucet, releasing clouds of billowing steam and filling the air with a moist, sticky warmth. The sink was full, water spilling over its sides and flowing down the porcelain like some artsy fountain, then streaming away across the tile, presumably according to some imperceptible tilt in the floor. It vanished down an open hallway, carpeted once again, slanting down at a steep angle from a corner of the room.

We walked over to the hallway to peer down. It was closer to vertical than horizontal, dropping at a vicious angle. Where the hot stream hit the tilted carpet it became black with mold, and the walls and ceiling of the tunnel were stained with rust and moss. Like water had been coursing through it for a long, long time.

From the slanting darkness rose a hot smell of rot.

"This feels different," Niko said.

We walked back to the sink and tried to turn off the faucet, but the hot and cold knobs spun loose. The scalding water rushed full force out of the tap, churning noisily in the basin.

"Gonna have a hell of a water bill," I joked, but then remembered something. The newspaper article from the history lady, about the old fort built on the site of our house. It had said something about a natural spring, an underground cavern.

Something felt on the verge of snapping into place, making sense. But I couldn't quite see it.

A looking-glass held above this stream
Will show your troubles like a dream

I dug through my pack and found a tiny mirror in the survival kit. You were supposed to use it to signal planes. I held it above the running water, angling it around, not sure what I expected to see.

There was nothing. Just the two of us, reflected back.

After a moment the billowing steam fogged the mirror, erasing the reflection.

I put it away, feeling deflated.

Niko was beaming his flashlight down the tunnel, chasing the descending path of the stream. "This would be rough going. Steep and slick. We'd need better climbing gear. And I can't see how far down it goes."

I took a deep breath. "It feels like that's the way, though. Doesn't it?"

He ran a hand through his hair, eyes still pulled down the shaft. "Jesus, I hope not."

I couldn't stop thinking about the wet tunnel as we retracted our steps. Images of it flashed through my mind. The thought of what might be past the reach of our flashlight beams, what was down there, was maddening. I was planning how soon we could come back down, what we'd have to bring with us. What it would take to keep pushing deeper.

For better or worse, we ended up missing the long twisting hallway on our way back. From the grid of rooms we found a different door that let out much closer to the bottom of our pit, and decided without too much discussion to take it. I was glad Niko didn't press the point. Maybe he'd forgotten.

I couldn't stand the thought of our perceptions of the world not agreeing.

We passed through the last few hallways to the base of shaft we'd come down. On the carpet directly underneath were our ropes, coiled up neat, Grip Monkeys still tied to the end.

"God damn it," Niko said with feeling, craning his head to glare accusingly at the shaft and fling curses up its length. We couldn't see anything unusual up there, not from down here.

Our way back up had been cut off.

We had extra grapples in our packs, but the originals didn't seem damaged: just detached. The shaft was too narrow to throw one all the way back up to the top without hitting a wall, so we settled for hooking a doorway, halfway up.

Our position now was much more precarious. We couldn't tell if the grapple was set properly: we just had to trust it. Niko volunteered to go first. From the ground below, I watched him climb, anxious.

He was a good climber. He made it to the sideways door without incident. From there, it was a matter of taking things in stages to get back up to the top. Each of the vertical rooms we passed served as a miniature base camp, a place to rest before flinging the grapple another few dozen feet to the next doorway. We'd both climb up and do it again. Eventually we made it back to the top. It was like a mountaineering expedition, kind of, except inside a house. So not at all, I suppose.

The camcorder was where we'd left it, sitting on the carpet pointed at the pit.

The door frame where the grapples had been attached wasn't damaged. We'd seated them pretty firmly, so this suggested that rather than being yanked free from below, someone had carefully unhooked them from up here.

Of course, the ropes had also been neatly coiled at the bottom. Someone had to have done that from down there.

Niko didn't want to watch the tape, not while we were still Downstairs. But I couldn't stand not knowing. So he huddled miserably beside me while we watched the footage on the tiny flip-out screen.

The tape had run to the end, so we backed it up a bit and hit play. To our dismay, the ropes were going over the edge right to the end; whatever happened, it had been after the tape ran out. Niko held down the rewind button and we settled in for a long haul. We spooled back through the whole tape, but nothing changed: it was two hours of motionless footage of the hallway and our ropes. Finally we saw ourselves spring back up from the pit at high speed, first me and then him; dicker with the grapples and rope, then zip over to the camera to turn it on. The tape clunked to a stop.

Cursing up a blue streak, Niko hit play. We watched in numb frustration as everything we'd done earlier played back: the same discussions about rope and seating the grapples, the same lame jokes failing to ease tension. There wasn't much point to watching it all unfold again. We just didn't know what else to do.

On the tiny screen, I was standing a pace or two back, wondering aloud how much stuff we should take down with us. I hated how my voice sounded on tape, how my face looked. I always had. Even on the tiny screen I could see red blotches. On the screen a miniature Niko sat on the edge of the pit, adjusting his ropes.

Distorted by the shitty camcorder speaker, he said, "How far down do you think this goes?"

My image shrugged, said "We should possibly go far deeper."

My skin crawled. "Oh my god."

Niko glanced at me. "What?"

"That's not what I said." My head was spinning. What *had* I said? Something like *It can't possibly go much deeper*, maybe. Not that.

Screen-Niko said "Yes, right. Actually, we shouldn't the two of us come back this route at all. No. We should go deeper and we should let's stay down, down and deep." His voice sounded strained, but he pulled his rope tight smartly. "Don't come back up until we find it, Ry. What it is we ought to find."

Where it gripped the camcorder, Niko's hand was pale. "I didn't say that either," he breathed. "I mean I said something about that long, some of those words and phrases maybe. But they're *different they're fucking different—*"

I shushed him, because the voices on the tape were speaking again. But now the words were familiar, mundane. We both watched the screen, afraid to blink, but nothing else seemed changed. Everything played out as we remembered. Except now every word and gesture caused a spike of uncertainty. *Had* I said that, exactly that? Had I moved my arm that way, stood in precisely that spot?

Screen-Niko started to rappel. The camera focused on my legs as I stood up top, watching him descend. On the screen I waited, then clipped onto the rope once he'd made it to the bottom.

Video Ryan checked his harness, took a deep breath, and started down.

He paused before his head dropped out of frame to call down to Niko: "Coming down." I remembered saying that.

Then he turned and looked straight at the camera.

Straight into the lens.

He held the gaze for a long moment.

Then glanced, deliberate, down the shaft. Then back to the camera.

Wide-eyed.

His head dropped out of sight.

We sat frozen, watching the video of the empty hall for a minute, two, the grainy image showing nothing but the empty hall and our ropes.

Niko breathed out. "Jesus." He closed the screen and sat the camera down, backing away from it like it was a bomb. "Jesus fucking Christ."

I kept staring at it. *A looking-glass held above this stream...*

"Jesus," he kept muttering. "Jesus."

We slept in the big room that night because we always had low-level headaches now when we went upstairs. We were becoming trolls, hiding from sounds, afraid to go out under the sky, only venturing from our cave to get more supplies, stock up for further ventures down. I slept under the foosball table, gathering dust. No one but us had been down here for weeks.

You won't be surprised to hear I had nightmares.

I replayed the tape in my dreams, over and over. Each time I rewound all the way to the start, intent to watch it through, to make sure there wasn't some clue I'd missed. And each time the tape was different. It was always Niko and the pit and I, but never the same. And whenever something changed, fresh dread flooded through me.

Sometimes the changes were slight, barely there, and I struggled to catch the altered words, the different glances. Sometimes our words were rearranged, as if to make cryptic cyphers, buried meanings on the verge of making sense but never quite resolving.

In some of these variations, Niko and I were boyfriends. A couple. I could tell from the words we used, the way we looked at each other. Nothing that would have been obvious to anyone but me. I replayed these scenes over and over, rewinding to catch the little glances, secret smiles.

There were other, worse versions.

There were dream-tapes where a gaunt Ryan and Niko fought each other for control of the camera, staring manic into the lens with frantic mouths full of rotting teeth, skin flaking beneath torn and faded rags sticky with dried blood, like they'd been trapped down there for months. They clawed at the lens, as if trying to climb into it. As if it somehow were a way back out.

There were tapes where we cursed out our watcher-selves, told them to go away, to never come back again, that what was down here would destroy us. There were others, far worse, where we smiled like wolves, invited ourselves to come down deep, and stay.

There were versions with two Nikos or two Ryans, pretending to be two different people. There were versions where we *were* different people, people I'd never seen. There were versions where we spoke other languages, or babbled idiot sounds and pretended they were speech.

There were versions where the carpet turned soft and we sunk into it like quicksand, Niko screaming while I smiled until fibers closed over my head. There were versions where hurricane winds sucked us screaming into the pit.

And on one tape—and I rewound and re-watched this over and over, in the dream—water from all the hallways poured into the pit, a four-sided waterfall. The carpets were black and sticky with moss trailing down into the vertical shaft, the air thick with steam. Something jostled the camera and it surged forward with the tide, water sloshing against the lens, until the scalding stream carried it over the edge and it fell, straight down into that boiling pit, surrounded by water on every side, gathering speed, falling into wet and steaming dark, faster and faster and faster...

I would jerk awake at this point, coated in sweat, and try not to fall back asleep. But when I did I'd find myself rewinding the tape yet again and pressing play, hoping this time the footage would return to normal. It was always changed, and I'd have to watch it all over from the beginning, hoping this version would show something useful, a hint, a clue, an answer.

$\gg 9 \ll$

I woke to the smell of stale nicotine. Niko leaned against the stairs back up to my room, staring into the dark, a lit cigarette between his fingers.

"Our lease says no smoking in here," I grunted, still shaking off nightmares.

He took another drag. "Blow me."

I laughed and he flashed me a wicked grin. It felt good to laugh. Even if it was a little bit forced, to make sure he knew that I knew he was kidding.

Rubbing my eyes, I sat up in my sleeping bag. After a moment I scrunched over beside him, back against the stairs.

We steeped in smoke and silence for a long minute.

"Did I ever tell you," he finally said, "about that time I went camping by myself, up in Brushwillow?" I shook my head. "Used to do that a lot, after the, uh. Accident."

I took that in. He hadn't brought it up in a long time. Neither had I.

"I went by myself, cause I didn't want a lot of people around just then, and it's easier than twisting people's arms to get them to come with you. Planning around schedules, all that bullshit." He shifted into citation voice. "'The man who goes alone can leave today, but the man who goes with others must wait until they're fucking ready.'"

"Yeah, Thoreau. I'm pretty sure he didn't cuss quite that

much, but something like that, yeah."

He shrugged. "I like it up there. Anyway."

I waited, staring into the whorled beige universe of the carpet.

"So this one night I'm up there, alone. I'm in my tent, and it's dark. Cloudy, no moon. I'm sleeping fine, on my back, you know, head up against the edge of the tent. And then I wake up, cause I hear something, just outside."

He sucked on the cigarette. "Something breathing. Low, hissing, gurgling breathing. Sounded huge, like a bear or something, a big-ass wolf. And it was right on the other side of the tent flap. Inches from my face. Like something had pressed its muzzle against the nylon, that thin nothing sheet of ultralight fabric, and was waiting.

"I still remember what that felt like. Fucking terrifying.

"I was too scared to move, so I lay there a long time, hoping it would go away. But it didn't. The thing stayed where it was. Kept making those horrible breathing sounds. Inhale. Exhale. Raspy, choking."

He flicked the cigarette onto the carpet, rubbed it out with his foot.

"And then I realized where the sound was coming from. The breathing was coming from me. I was sleeping on a root or something, my head had gotten into some funny angle. I was snoring, basically, and woke myself up. But I didn't realize what woke me was a sound I was making myself."

"Okay." I rubbed a hand over my face, tried to think. "You're saying maybe there's not... a *thing* down there. That somehow, all of it is us."

"Echoes," he said. "Reflections. The rooms are reflections of our shitty old house, and the things we're seeing, experiencing down there, maybe they're not alive. We're causing them, somehow. And now we're ascribing intentionality to side effects. Jumping at our own shadows." He lay back down on his sleeping bag, staring up at the ceiling.

I remembered something from a neurobiology class. "Did you know there are more neurons going from your brain to your eyes than in the other direction?"

"So?"

"From your brain to your eyes," I repeated, "not the other way around."

He blinked. "That doesn't make sense."

"It does if you realize that vision is mostly the brain telling the eyes what it expects them to see." I rubbed my face again, trying to wipe off the exhaustion. "We think we have two little cameras in our head. We don't. They're little yes-men, reassuring us nothing unexpected is happening. That's why that trick works, with the guy in the gorilla suit. You ever see that video in school?"

He nodded. "You're watching a bunch of people toss a ball around, and the guy in the gorilla suit walks right through them, and it's like he's invisible. He even waves. But you don't see him the first time, because you're watching the ball. Then you watch it again looking for him and your mind's blown." He smiled faintly. "Dude in my high school science class swore the teacher changed the tape."

"You don't see the gorilla because you don't expect to. There's no reason he'd be there, so your eyes don't notice him. Even though he's in plain sight. Standing right in front of you."

We were both quiet for a while.

"So maybe we're somehow looking at this wrong," I finally said. "We're not seeing something. We keep saying it doesn't make any sense. Maybe we're just not seeing it the right way."

"Maybe." He closed his eyes. "Or maybe there's nothing there to see."

"Niko. About the accident." I swallowed. "That night."

He rolled over. "Don't want to talk about it."

"I know. But if you ever did want to, I mean, if you ever needed that again—"

"I don't. Go the fuck to sleep, man."

We both closed our eyes and tried. I could feel the camcorder dream lingering, eager to take over again. I tried to fight it off, but I was so tired.

"Even if we are the wolf," Niko muttered, just as I was about to drift off, "that doesn't mean it's not trying to kill us."

I got fired from my job, which was fair enough; I'd missed two shifts in the past week. I got a nosebleed during the meeting with my supervisor. He told me to go home and take care of myself. I was halfway home before I remembered that phrase has a positive meaning, too.

I'd thought he was telling me to commit suicide.

Something was in my room when I got back. I stood outside the closed door, dried blood on my face, listening. It sounded like an elephant. Heavy, clopping footfalls made the floorboards groan. Wet, agitated breathing rasped. Dust motes danced at my feet in a strange breeze, sucked under and pushed back out through the space below the closed door, rhythmic. Air moved with faint fleshy sounds, like a hundred quiet people flapping their arms, flailing.

I crept away, miserable, and by the time I came back with Niko and he threw open the door in some play at courage, there was nothing there.

I collapsed into his arms, sobbing, and he let me stay there for a while until I'd calmed down. I clung to him, afraid if I loosened my grip he'd disappear.

He had a perpetual headache now. He kept describing it with the word "throbbing" and only that word, as if clinging to the sound of it. Like using a different one would acknowledge the pain too had changed, grown worse, was no longer caged by the word he'd picked to trap it. I could see how much it hurt him to think, to make words, to move around. He ground his teeth. He was being worn down.

My headaches were getting worse, too, but it wasn't the pain that bothered me. It was the strain of always having them that wore on me. Of wondering if I'd have them for the rest of my life.

We left to explore down the slippery tunnel late that night. It might have made more sense to go down after a good night's rest, but neither of us could sleep, and spending so much time down there meant night and day were becoming academic concepts anyway. Niko caffeined up (I was jittery enough already), and we loaded our packs with canned food and power bars, thick gloves, and crampons from the sporting goods store. "12 points of contact ensures solid grip on ice," the box had said. We didn't expect the manufacturer had tested them on moldy carpet, but it was the best we could do.

In my pack was also a gun. I bought it from a place I'd driven past every day on my way to work but never gone into until that morning. The friendly clerk agreed to waive the mandatory waiting period in exchange for the last of my ATM cash. I didn't tell Niko about the gun. I thought it would make me feel safer but it just felt heavy.

It had been a hot day and the old house clung to that heat through the night with grim brick desperation. Descending into chillier air was a relief. With every step down the headaches diminished, our mood improved. It was almost addictive, being down there.

We retraced our route through the upper halls to the top of the shaft and reset the grapples. This time Niko hammered them into the doorjamb, face set, until he'd driven the steel spikes three inches into the wood. Even so, neither of us really expected they'd still be there when we got back.

When, or if.

Getting down was a familiar exercise now, danger mitigated by procedure and repetition. We retraced our route to the tiled room with the sink via the shortcut we'd found. The water was still running, hot and steaming, rushing across the floor to the corner with its angled hallway lined with slimy black carpet. We shined our lights down the hot throat and the steam grabbed their brightness, bounced it back to us maliciously. We couldn't see more than a few body lengths down.

Niko ran a hand through his curls, deflating again in the hot moist air; scratched the hair behind his ear furiously, like a dog with an itch. He was shaking. "Are we sure about this? Really really? Because it sort of seems like a colossally stupid thing to do."

"You have a better idea?"

He sighed, looking down the steaming shaft unhappily.

"No, I don't have a better idea," he said at last.

We pulled on the crampons and the heavy gloves. Harness, rope, knots. Check. Niko pounded two new Grip Monkeys into either side of the angled tunnel entrance. We tied on. Double-check.

Then, each holding our rope, kicking hard to sink the sharp toes of the crampons deep into the slimy carpet, we started down.

It was slow, hot work. Once we got inside the slanted hall, the steam was oppressive, everywhere: we were instantly drenched with it, like rot-smelling sweat. Even with the crampons our feet slipped. The sludge was deep and slick, a stew of algae and mold and fungal slimes, green-black and stinking of putrefying jungle, of horrible things happening under your carpet, inside your walls. We held tight to the ropes with steam-wet gloves. The walls and floor twisted and bent as we descended, as if the constant moisture had warped them, but the downward angle stayed relentless.

It was a gullet. We were letting ourselves be swallowed. No— worse. We were forcing ourselves in. Eager. Like we couldn't wait to be digested.

We were nearing the end of our sixty meter ropes when everything went to shit.

All at once we were sliding. Our ropes had gone slack in our hands, no longer connected to anything. There was no time to dig in the crampons; we were already moving too fast, careening down like a grotesque slalom. Neither of us screamed, focused I guess on trying to grab hold of something, anything, but there were no doorways, no light fixtures, nothing but the thick hot slime and the scalding water. I tried to dig my feet into the oozing carpet but my loose rope had entangled me, my pack was in my way, my face was smeared with scalding gunk and I couldn't open my eyes.

My hand closed on Niko's leg and I grabbed it. A moment later the floor angle shifted and he cried out, threw his body sideways, brought us both to a shuddering, squelchy stop.

We were soaked through, overheating. Scalding water ran past us down the slope. I blinked my eyes open and saw he'd wedged himself into a kink in the tunnel. One of his knees was scraped open and a dull red mark on his forehead was beginning to swell. But he'd done it. He'd stopped us.

Ropes slithered down the tunnel past us, followed moments later by two grapples still tied to their ends. Niko reached out to grab one with his free hand, but his weight shifted, and he had to throw the hand back against a wall to re-brace, cursing. I tried to snag them with my foot, but didn't even come close. They vanished down the tunnel, trailing rope.

Niko's face was tight. He tilted his head down toward me. "This was a mistake. God, we're so fucking stupid. Ryan, man. We have to go back."

"Calm down," I gasped, head filled with the roaring of the water, blinking gunk from my eyes. "Don't panic. We can do this."

"Man, I'm barely holding on. I don't know how much longer I can keep from slipping. We have to try to climb back up."

"Back?" I said, confused. "You want to go back?"

He stared down at me. "Of course back. Are you fucking

crazy? Where the fuck else?"

"There's nothing good up there. Nothing right." I kicked my foot for purchase, managed to rest at least some weight on a hidden protuberance. "Besides, nothing's changed. The plan's still the same."

"Are you not paying attention?" he hissed, furious. "Something is trying to kill us."

"So let's figure out how to stop it." I tried to keep my tone reasonable. "We're halfway down already. Climbing back up will be hard, regardless. Why not get all the way to the bottom first?"

"Because we don't even know if there is a bottom." His face was blotched red with fury, with sweat, with the scorching heat of the air. "Halfway? We have no fucking idea how deep this goes. I should have said this a long time ago. You're obsessed. You get obsessed a lot, man, let it drag you down. Your stupid records." He took a deep breath. "Well now you're obsessed with this place, and it's blinding you. It's *feeding* on you, your obsessions. Multiplying them. You can't see it, or maybe you don't want to, but I do. I'm looking right at it. Like the gorilla in the crowd."

I was angry. "If I'm obsessed with anything, it's with finding a way back. We're running out of time. We either figure this out, or we're stuck here forever, in the wrong world. We need each other to get through this." I said it again, like saying it could make it true. "We need each other."

"You're obsessed with me, too," he muttered. "When was the last time you hung out with someone else?"

"When was the last time you did?"

He shook his head angrily, dismissing this.

"Our housemates," I pushed, "when was the last time you hung out with any of them? Anyone other than me?" He stared back, seething. "Their names. I bet you can't even remember their names." I was bluffing. But could I remember them, either? Names, faces. No. There was nothing. None of those people mattered, not to me, not to us. We were the only thing that mattered. Getting back to where we'd been, what we'd had. What I'd wanted.

He shook his head again, violent, like there was something inside it he wanted to dislodge. "You're living in a fantasy," he spat, "you always have been. *I can't be what you want me to be, okay?* I can't be what anyone fucking wants me to be. You all have these versions of me in your head, these ideal perfect Nikos, but they're not real. They're not real. I can't live up to them." He opened his eyes, stared yearningly back up the shaft. "Help me. If you really care about me, help me back up. Don't be like everyone else. Don't just fucking *use* me to get what you want."

"Going back's not going to help. There's no answers up there." He wasn't understanding. I reached for something else. "Those headaches aren't going away. You think you can live with that pain? Forever?"

"Better than being fucking dead!" He seemed to realize I wasn't changing my mind, turned away to reach for a handhold, but there was nothing there, nothing to grip, and he scrabbled pathetically at the slime.

"Is it?" I shouted, angry, desperate. I had to say something, something that would make him stay, keep him here, and my mouth raced ahead of me. "You won't make it, up there, not with pain like that. We both know you won't."

He tensed, glared down at me. "What the fuck is that supposed to mean?"

"You know exactly what it means," I said, shaking. "Never really helped you. I've done nothing but help you. I've always been there for you. Every fucking time you fall I pick you back up. *You'd be dead if it weren't for me.*"

He shot me with a gaze of such cold fury I cringed. "You're fucking poison," he hissed, "you know that? A fucking snake. I wish you'd let me die that night. I wish we'd never met. *Let go of me!*"

And his hand did close on something, and he pulled himself up, triumphant. His leg was slipping out of my hands, and I couldn't bear for him to crawl away from me, couldn't handle the thought of going back up to that world, to any world where everything was wrong and nothing I wanted was possible, so I pulled. I pulled, too hard, and both his hands slipped, and he crashed back into me, only I wasn't holding onto anything but him any more so both of us tumbled down, faster and faster, slipping and twisting and scraping together down the steepening blood-hot slope, down and down and down into darkness.

PART TWO

MULTIPLICIOUS

We two boys together clinging,
One the other never leaving

Walt Whitman

≫ 10 ≪

The first time someone kissed me it didn't really count.

I'm in the closet at the back of the band room, sophomore year of high school, and this annoying girl, Missy or Misty or something, has followed me in to grab the music stands, and she's especially giggly and flighty and nervous for some reason, brushing up against me, and then the lights switch off and she grabs me and I realize it's a setup, she got someone to stay out there and flip the switch: and in the sudden gloom she grabs me and crushes her lips against mine. And all I can think of in this moment is all the guys this could have been, friends I'd been too shy to get close to, guys from the showers or the seat across from me in homeroom, even guys who brushed past me in the hall with a glance and made me crazy for the rest of the day. Three months later I'd meet Bradley and have a real first kiss and all would be forgotten, brushed aside in favor of a thousand better kisses, remembered still despite the awful way they ended. But now in the closet as this dumb girl's lips push against mine all I can think of is what's been taken from me, the legend of my first kiss, how I've fucked it up, lost it, failed some future boy and myself and even this girl, whose eyes I can't meet as I pull away and brush past her out of the closet and past snickering faces to the door outside, changed, maybe, or maybe not. Her hair was in the way, after all, long straight blonde strands of it tasting like strawberry conditioner, so our lips didn't really even

119

touch, let alone tongues. Was that a kiss? Did it count? Who knows. I don't feel like it should, and anyway I don't feel any different except maybe worse, somewhere deep down, even less experienced and less ready and less sure of who I'm supposed to be. I drop out of band not long after that. I've always liked listening to music more than playing it, anyway, and I like to listen alone.

I plunged into a pool of steaming hot water, instantly immersed, choking. My scrabbling hand found something slimy but solid and pushed against it. My face broke the surface and I gasped, slipping and struggling to my feet. Water came up to my waist. I wiped rank muck off my face, blinked burning eyes open, tried to catch my breath.

It was utterly dark. All I could hear was splashing water.

"Niko?" I shouted.

Nothing.

I shrugged off my pack, zipped it open with blind, shaking fingers while struggling to keep it above the waterline, and fumbled around inside. My hand closed on a plastic tube. Glowstick. I pulled it out and snapped it, shook it, frantic.

A dim blue glow began to bring the world back, a breath at a time. Churning water was everywhere, white and frothy. Steam swayed. Above my head a sheer shaft opened up and angled away, lined in oozing black gunk and coursing fluid. The one we'd slid down, presumably. Turning all the way around, the edges of my dim circle of light suggested level hallways, flooded, leading off into darkness in three equidistant directions.

No sign of Niko.

Something dark and coiling swirled in the water: my rope. I grabbed for it and reeled it in. One end was still attached to my waist. At the end of the other, my shiny grappling hook trailed tangled green streamers.

I searched the frothing surface, but saw no sign of a second grapple, or a second rope.

Shutting my eyes, I tried to sort through the confusion of the sliding fall. We had tumbled, together at first, my hands grabbing for his slime-drenched shirt, the sodden edges of his pack. But there was nothing to get a grip on. After those first few moments all I could feel was my own tangled rope, the pasty mulch sliding past me. I assumed I'd gotten ahead of him, or behind.

But what if I hadn't? What if he'd managed to stop himself again behind me, wedged himself into another kink in the tunnel?

Or what if the tunnel had split, somewhere up there?

I didn't want to think about the third possibility, but I spent a few grim minutes duck-walking through the water, old rescue swim lessons running through my head, feeling my hands through the muck beneath the churning surface. I found nothing solid. No backpack, no rope. No body.

He wasn't here. I was alone.

Everything in my pack was soaked. I threw out a waterlogged sandwich and watched it drift in the churning current before vanishing beneath the foam, as if someone hungry underneath had grabbed it. I'd lost a crampon in the fall and couldn't find it, so I took off the other one and maneuvered it into my pack. The blue light from the glowstick turned everything the same shades. Black and blue.

I had no idea if the dripping gun would still work, and was seized by a thick fear now of firing it down here—of how far that sound would carry and what it might attract—but I slipped it into my belt anyway. It still didn't make me feel safe but I tried to pretend it did.

My flashlight wouldn't turn on, even with fresh batteries. "Water resistant," according to the package, but I imagined it had been subjected to an environment outside factory test conditions. I strapped it to the top of my pack anyway, hoping it might dry out and be useful again. I had a dozen waterproof glowsticks, so I wasn't really worried about light.

Not yet, anyway.

I stared up the shaft we'd tumbled down for a long time, considering. Climbing back up—without a rope, with only one crampon, without someone helping me—seemed impossible. I tried to picture Niko up there somewhere, struggling to pull himself back up, handhold by slippery handhold. If he made it to the top, he'd throw another rope down to me.

Wouldn't he?

I waited a long time, as long as I could stand it. It might have only been a few hours, maybe even less. But it grew more and more maddening to simply stand there, soaked through, bathed in steam and sweat, doing nothing. Wondering if he was trying to find me. Wondering if he'd left me behind. Wondering if he was drowning or dead or lost, somewhere in this irrational maze.

At last I decided to move. If he'd made it back up, he could take care of himself. And if he was down here somewhere, maybe I could find him. Anyway hadn't I said it would be silly to make it all the way here and not explore?

It was the deepest we'd been yet. Maybe there were answers down here. Or at least another way out.

I picked a flooded hallway, took out my keys and gouged a crude arrow into the shitty paint of the wall, drywall dust spilling out. Breadcrumbs, to find my way back. Or show Niko where I'd gone, if he was lost down here too, or came looking for me.

And if something else comes looking, you're pointing it right at you.

But there was nothing to be done about that. I gave the shaft back up one last doleful look, then turned to the hallway and began to push my way forward through the hot, sluggish water.

I wandered. I'm not sure for how long. The black water's surface smoothed once I moved away from the turbulence at the bottom of the shaft, swallowed up the glowstick's dim blue light. There were no longer any curious features or unusual architecture: only an irregular grid of junctions. The infrequent side rooms were either empty or filled with rotting furniture floating on the surface, waterlogged, ruined. Sometimes the floor or ceiling sloped up or down, not always in sync; so the water level would drift from ankle-deep to above my waist, and the ceiling from claustrophically low to beyond the reach of my light. The halls trended wider and narrower, too, in unpredictable rhythms. I worried for a while about stepping into a pit I couldn't see and dunking myself again, but there weren't any. Nor were there stairs, up or down, or even light fixtures. Only hallways, branching, recombining, endless.

The air stayed steamy, and while the water cooled as I moved farther from the hot inlet stream it was still uncomfortably warm. I felt hot and clammy, thick-headed. Mist swirled in the air, sculpting the dim blue light into strange shapes and shadows.

I kept gouging arrows into the wall with a key, kept moving. If I kept moving I wouldn't have to stop, wouldn't have to think.

Walking takes almost no thinking at all.

I came to another spot where the hallway widened, but this was different. Running along the indentation in one wall was a row of pay phones.

I slowed to a stop and stared, wondering if they were really there.

They rose from knee-deep water, six of them each on its own steel pole. The ceiling had risen so high my glowstick couldn't find it, but light stabbed down from somewhere, spotlighting each phone fierce and bright after hours of flat blue glow.

Water sloshed as I trudged over to the nearest phone, reluctant but intrigued. Pay phones don't normally live inside a house. Did that mean something?

I touched the black plastic of the receiver. It felt grimy and cold. As if in a dream, I lifted it, held it to my ear.

Dial tone.

I blinked as it droned in my ear. This didn't make sense. If there was no power this far down, surely there weren't phone lines either. Some telecom grunt hadn't run a cable all the way down here, snaking it through all these endless halls and vertical shafts, had they? Hope they billed by the hour.

The sound of the dial tone was uncomfortably familiar.

Without meaning to, I reached out a finger and dialed a number from an old commercial jingle. Seven sing-song digits.

A voice told me to insert fifty cents.

I almost laughed at this familiar banality. I slapped my pockets, but had no change. I hadn't expected to need any.

I put down the receiver, lifted it again and dialed zero, still not really expecting anything would happen.

A ring, and then a woman's voice: "Operator."

My bluff had been called. I didn't know what to say. "Er... I'd, uh, like to make a collect call."

"Please hang up, dial star nine seven, then the number you wish to call. Say your name at the first tone."

"Thanks," I managed.

She was gone. The silence hung oppressive in her absence. I needed a voice back on that line. With a couple words she'd made the familiar loneliness unbearable.

But who could I call? Water sloshed around my knees as I considered the utter inexplicability of my situation. Should I call the police, explain I was lost in my own basement, miles from the surface? Ask the fire department to send a rescue team through my bed, down the vertical hallway, and throw a rope ladder into the slimy tube in the giant bathroom?

Or maybe I'd call a friend. You know, one who'd believe me, who wouldn't hang up thirty seconds into my story. In the movies, whenever someone says "You wouldn't believe me if I told you," there's always someone to say back: "Try me." This person invariably turns out to be surprisingly open-minded.

I knew with grim certainty this was not going to work for

me. The only friend I had like that was Niko. And he was gone.

I felt desperately alone.

My fingers brushed against the dial pad, hesitating. They punched star nine seven and then kept going, tracing out a familiar pattern, a groove deep in muscle memory. My fingers knew it well.

At the first tone, I said my name.

Something clicked and whirred in the receiver. A pause, and then, a ring.

Another.

Another.

Someone picked up and said, "Hello?"

"Mom." Relief flooded through me like adrenaline. You trust a voice like that on a primitive level, instinctual, in parts of your brain deeper than logic, than thought.

She must have heard something in my tone. "Honey? What's wrong?"

"What, I only call you when something's wrong?" But my eyes were tearing up and my hands were trembling. I held the phone tight against my face. It smelled like old sweat and institutional cleaner.

With my other hand I wiped my forehead. Swallowed. "Nothing's wrong. Just wanted to hear your voice. How are things? Tell me what you're up to." I didn't care what she said. I only wanted her to talk and keep on talking. To hear sounds from a normal world and pretend I was part of it. That I'd ever been part of it.

She humored me for a minute, but I could tell she was worried. And I could think of nothing to say that would get me out of here.

"Alright, star man," she finally said, and my brain flashed to my sixth birthday when she dressed up like an astronaut to bring in my cake. Crêpe paper planets and glow-in-the-dark comets. "Fess up. What's going on?"

"I'm... I'm in trouble, mom." My voice was breaking. "Something's happened. You remember my... my friend Niko?" I rushed forward, babbling. "I've lost him, mom, I don't know where he is, where either of us are. I fucked things up and I don't know what to do. This is too big, all of this is too big, and I... I made a mistake, and..." I bit my lip so I'd stop talking, something pressing down hard on my chest, and gripped the phone like it was my last anchor to reality. Maybe it was.

She took a deep breath. Let it out.

"Oh, honey," she said. "Is it... is it AIDS?"

Of all the things to be terrified about right then, that one was so far down the list that my brain sort of tripped over itself, downshifted straight back to first and stalled the hell out. "Oh," I said. "Uh. What? No. No, it's not AIDS. Mom. I wouldn't tell you something like that over the phone." I took a deep breath, and once again said something I probably shouldn't have. I said it with deadly seriousness. "It's HIV."

There was an awful silence.

Then I started giggling. I couldn't help myself. "That's not funny, Orion," she said, but then she was laughing too, and neither of us could stop, even when she kept trying to, kept saying "Orion" again in her serious voice which just set me off more, which set her off again too. And if I could have given anything to stretch that moment out forever, I'd have done it in a heartbeat.

I wiped tears from the corners of my eyes. "I'm sorry. No, it's not that. I can't really explain it. I guess I just needed to hear your voice more than anything. I'll... figure something out."

"That's my smartie." I could picture her expression when she said this; she'd said it a lot. "You're sure it's nothing I can help with?"

"I'm sure." The blue monochrome of the glowstick made the pay phone into an artsy abstraction; the blackness around me sucked away all the rest of its light.

"Well, you'll figure it out. You always have, even when...

when there wasn't someone there to help you." She took a deep breath. That was a big thing for her to admit. "You know you can always ask for help when you need to. But you won't always need to. And that's okay."

Tears were pushing out of my eyes again, damn it. I leaned against the booth, screwing them shut. "Thanks, mom," I whispered.

"I love you, sweetie," she said. "Do you want to talk to Bradley?"

And out of everything that had happened, all the unexplained and terrifying and gut-wrenching things, nothing hit me like those words did. Sometimes words hit harder than a slap. You feel them, like ten thousand volts. They sour everything that came before, ruin everything coming after. That's how those words hit me.

"What?" I managed, my voice small.

"He was helping us shop for your sister's prom, remember? The three of us had a blast. Hang on, I'll put him on."

I stood clutching the phone, unable to move, to breathe.

Faint rustling sounds came over the line.

"Hey, gorgeous."

There are some voices you hope you'll never hear again. When a person bends you so far you snap, you can usually forget about the piece of you that broke off, until something reminds you of the splintered edge where more of you used to be. When people die or move away or betray you and you tuck your thoughts of them out of sight like a forgotten photo album, it's a shock when the book is dragged back out, the pages wrenched open, frozen moments shoved unwanted toward your face.

The stylus of a record player is a needle, dragged along a ragged surface to conjure ghosts of long-ago sounds: instruments, rhythms. Voices. If you don't consent to be played, the needle hurts.

"Brad." I didn't know what else to say.

"You will not believe this dress we found for Sarah." I could hear his mischievous smile, the sound of the glints in his eyes. His tone was light and playful and casual. Like we'd last spoken yesterday. Like nothing had ever been wrong.

"Brad," I said again, "what the fuck are you doing at my mom's house?"

"Oh, you know, casing the joint," he said breezily. "Your mom has a lot of good stuff. Is it okay if I just say 'mom?' *She's* been saying My Second Son all day, so it's kind of awkward if I don't. Oh my god, Orion, does she know something I don't?"

"What?" I felt weak.

"This mysterious camping trip," he teased. "Wanting everything to be perfect. Don't worry, babe, I'm good at pretending to be surprised."

"What are you talking about?" I sounded like an idiot but I couldn't help myself. Nothing made sense. This conversation was out of its groove, the needle scratching across the surface, leaving an ugly mark that could never be buffed out.

How could he act like everything was fine, after all that had happened? Like any of this was normal?

Maybe in this universe, it was.

This had never once occurred to me since I'd passed through to this side. It was too huge a change. All the differences were so tiny, so inconsequential. Not like this.

I couldn't conceive of what my life would have been like, if we'd never inscribed those wounds on each other. If we'd stayed whole. Who would I even have become? Who would he?

Or.

Maybe it's not him at all.

Something inside me withdrew, to wherever small animals go in their heads while staring down looming headlights. Some residual part of me thought I ought to move, speak, react. Get out of the way. But I didn't know how.

"So is this super-secret message part of the whole thing?" He still sounded playful, flirty. "All this stuff about *going deeper*?"

My blood was frozen and my mouth had gone dry. "What?"

"When you called last night," he explained, voice still achingly familiar, "so secretive. You said next time we talked I was supposed to remind you that you need to go deeper." I could hear him raising his eyebrows, somehow, seductive. "I'm not opposed, dear, although maybe we shouldn't talk about this"—he dropped into a stage whisper—"when your mother's in the other room."

"I didn't talk to you yesterday."

The ground felt like it was dropping away.

"I wrote it down because it was so weird." I could hear the rustle of a paper: I could see him, squinting through his glasses. "I'm supposed to say that you're not deep enough yet, and you need to keep going down. Deeper and deeper. As deep as you can get." He cleared his throat meaningfully. "I mean you know I'm all for going down in general, babe, but seriously, what's the deal?"

"I don't... I can't..." There were so many things I wanted to say to him. Fear and anger and a homesick longing for places that can't be returned to were churning around inside me. I couldn't accept this. I didn't know if I could even survive it.

"Babe," he said, "what's wrong? You're being weird."

"I loved you," I whispered.

"I love you, too," he said, mishearing, and then something spasmed inside me, my lungs locking up like in a cramp, refusing to breathe. My vision closed down to a tunnel. My fingers went numb.

I dropped the phone. It swung on the end of its metal coil, spinning slowly. I could still hear his voice, faint and distorted—

"Ryan?"

—Bradley's voice, drifting faint from those tiny holes in the receiver, as I backed away, staring—

"Orion? You there?"

—and my shoulders hit the wall, and I couldn't back away any more but I could still hear his voice coming out of the receiver, so I pulled out my gun and shot it.

Somehow I hit the dangling receiver on my first shot, and it exploded. Tiny bits of plastic shrapnel cut the air. One whizzed past my cheek and sliced it open. I didn't notice. I raised the gun to the boxy metal body of the phone and shot that, too. I shot it again and again until the gun wouldn't fire any more.

My ears hurt. The reverberations were deafening, echoing endlessly. I pictured compressed sound waves expanding through miles of hallways, like a dangerous thought lighting up more and more neurons, bouncing off skullbone to keep reflecting, multiplying, feeding on itself. A sound crashing up staircases and down shafts in rippling patterns of interference and reinforcement. I stared down at the gun in my hand, thoughts dull, shots ringing and echoing in my head and through the halls. I unclenched my hand and the gun fell into the water, vanishing under the surface without a splash.

The phone made a distinct, metallic *clunk.*

I looked up at its bullet-riddled surface.

Inside, something was tumbling down through the pay phone's innards, dinging and plinking past metal obstructions. My gaze moved down, following its invisible path through the body of the phone.

Finally, the clattering stopped. The gate of the coin return jiggled as something clunked into the slot behind it.

Not wanting to, I edged forward. Part of me reached out while another part tried in horror to call my hand back, but it kept moving. It pushed the gate open.

In the coin return was a small brass key.

I stared at it for a long moment. Then I snatched the key and pulled back, turning away from the bank of phones in the same movement. I slogged fiercely on through the water and down the hall, moving fast, not looking back.

My ears still rang with gunshots. In the silence, that ring kept sounding almost like a distant telephone, bell clanging some-where far behind me. I tried to ignore them, but the ghost sounds didn't fade for hours.

≫ 11 ≪

In a flooded side room half the floor had given way. Water cascaded down into consuming blackness, no lower level visible. I stepped carefully past the open door and the strong current rushing in, tide sucking my shins like it was hungry for them, and sloshed away fast up the hall, shuddering at the thought of that black pit. You fell into that thing, God knows where you'd land.

Soon after, the hall began sloping up. The carpet went from wet to merely damp, and then, between one step and the next, dry.

Up ahead glimmered a tiny spark of yellow. I stumbled closer: a night-light, plugged into an outlet at the base of the wall. Something about it whispered of lightning bugs and sleepy summer nights, and all at once I felt immensely weary. I fell to my knees when I reached the weak light and sloughed off my waterlogged pack, then curled up around the tiny pale glow as if it was a campfire. My face snuggled into the brown whorls of the carpet like the fur of some huge indifferent beast. I slept.

My body did, anyway. My mind kept marching.

I dreamed endless waterlogged halls. I trudged, not making any attempt to mark my way or track my position. I searched for nothing, found nothing: just wandered. When I realized I was dreaming I tried to break free of the nightmare, think of anything else, but lucidity was slippery, fumbled away between heartbeats, and I kept losing it. I walked halls lit only by flickering sea-blue light and thought of nothing that wasn't them.

Once, in a long, straight hall of waist-deep water that never seemed to end, the surface ahead of me shifted, swirled.

Something moved underneath.

I stopped short, squinting, and held my glowstick high. The ripples flung its dim light back to me, bunched up and distorted. But it was enough to see something person-shaped under the surface, swimming toward me.

The gun was in my hand: in this dream, I'd forgotten I lost it. Gripped by fear, I aimed it at the thing under the surface and pulled the trigger. But the shots went wide, from the angle of the water or some grim nightmare-logic. Whatever it was kept coming.

I cringed back against the wall. The thing beneath the water was doing the breaststroke with smooth, efficient moves. It didn't break the surface and it never came up for air. Through the rippled distortions I could see no face.

But as it swam past, ignoring me, I could see it wore my clothes.

It didn't slow down. I pressed my back against the wall, cold sweat prickling my face, helpless to stop my head turning to watch it pass.

It swam to the end of the hall and around a corner, never stopping for breath, leaving a wake of dark whorls and eddies.

I woke with a parched, sticky mouth. My face was glued to the carpet with dried blood from where the piece of phone had cut my cheek. I tugged myself free, which reopened the cut. Wincing, I sat up and rummaged in my waterlogged pack for something to staunch the bleeding, still half-asleep. I'd left my soaked shoes on and my feet felt like they'd swelled to twice their normal size inside them.

My glowstick had long since burnt out. The nightlight's weak yellow glow reduced the world to a dim circle of carpet, a few feet across. And I was groggy, still shaking dream-remnants from my head. So I didn't realize until I started digging for a fresh glowstick that someone was sitting a few feet away.

I gasped and leapt up, scrabbling back against the wall behind me. I could see only tennis shoes, catching the amber edge of the nightlight, and the faintest hint of a body in the shadows behind them, knees pulled up with clasping hands. Someone sitting with their back against the wall, faint yellow glints in two eyes. Watching.

I stayed there trembling for a moment, too afraid to either come closer or flee into the blackness back the way I'd come. I'd left my pack in the circle of light, between me and whoever was sitting beyond it.

I realized I recognized the shoes.

Hesitant, I cleared my throat. "Niko?"

The face was so shadowed I could barely make it out, but I thought it smiled. "Hey, man."

The voice was cracked, weak. But familiar. Unmistakable.

I stepped back toward the light. "Shit, dude, you scared me." He made no move to get up. "What happened to you? We got separated and I didn't know what to do. Did you hear my gunshots? Jesus, I'm glad you're okay."

I knelt and pulled a new glowstick from my pack, but he held up a hand.

"Okay if we talk for a minute first, like this?" he said. "Been in the dark for fucking ever and that thing will murder my eyes." He lowered the hand. "Cool?"

It was such a relief to hear his voice again I shoved the glow-stick back down, along with a vague sense of unease. "Fine. So what happened?"

"Rather hear what happened to you. Tell me everything."

So I did. How I'd waited at the bottom of the shaft, explored the water-soaked hallways. I told him about the call at the bank of payphones. But I left out the part with the gun, because in hindsight it felt stupid, and because I remembered he didn't know about the gun, and I didn't want to mar our reunion by revealing I'd kept something from him. Something else, anyway.

He didn't say much. The yellow glints bobbed at times like he was nodding or cocking his head. But the darkness was fierce. All I could really make out were his shoes, and the hands clasped around his knees. In the pale yellow of the night-light they looked skeletal, emaciated.

Disquiet crept into me, rising through the floor into my feet and up my bones. I couldn't see his face. I wanted to.

"Hey," I finally said, "this dark is kind of freaking me out. You can shield your eyes or whatever, but I've got to have some light. Okay?"

He sighed, as if resigned. "If you have to."

I reached carefully for a glowstick the same way I used to walk deliberately towards the light switch in my childhood basement, shepherding growing panic with a forced front of calm. I pulled one out, snapped it, shook it, blinked at the surge of orange light from mingling chemicals, and held it up, anxious, as the light crept toward him.

The electric orange was shockingly bright, and he'd winced and held up a hand to block it out. He kept it there for a long moment as I squinted, pupils squirming. Finally, almost reluctant, he dropped the hand and met my gaze, defiant.

Something was wrong with him.

He was changed. Distorted. Something had leathered him, shrunken and withered his features, hollowed his eye sockets. At first he seemed like some poorly made caricature, face a twisted copy of the one I knew so well. But then I started to realize what had happened to him.

Time.

He was older. Much older.

I was still in the shallows of my twenties, remember. I hadn't been around long enough to see how age inscribes itself on people, crumples parents into grandparents and invalids and corpses. I hadn't seen friends lose hair and teeth and muscle tone. I hadn't loved someone long enough to find out what decades do to them.

The Niko against the wall looked twice as old as he should have been, maybe more. He was wearing different clothes, but out of his standard wardrobe: the bowling shirt with "My Name Is BONG" on the lapel. It wasn't threadbare or faded. Something bulged from the front pocket, maybe a penlight, and his pack leaned against the wall beside him.

He held my gaze, waiting. We stared at each other for a long time.

"What happened?" I finally said.

He took a breath. Let it out. "You can see what happened." He cleared his throat. I realized now he wasn't tired, or strained. His voice was just older. "So. Yeah. I'm not your Niko, man. Okay?"

I stiffened. "You're... from the other side?"

He smiled. "Ah. You still think there's just two sides. Sure, course you do." He shook his head. "Guess that's how it seems near the surface. A pair of possibilities. Neat. But deeper down, things get more... *tangled.*" The word sounded heavy in his throat, dangerous.

"What do you mean?" I couldn't stop staring at him, at his face, and I swayed with the sick feeling of recognition and strangeness, curdled together by that fierce orange light.

"There's a lot of space down here, Orion. A lot of... possibilities. Most of them aren't good." His glance had drifted down the corridor, but now it snapped back to my face. "*My* Ryan and I, we got lost. Long time ago. Real fucking lost. We, uh. Never made it back."

"Your Ryan?" I looked around, panic spiking. "There's some older version of me down here too?"

He looked away. "No."

After a moment, I realized he wasn't going to say anything else. And then why.

His eyes flicked back to mine again, as if fascinated by them. He stared with something like hunger. At seeing my face again? At seeing anyone?

"Been on my own a long time," he said, as if explaining. "Gotten used to it."

Suddenly I couldn't accept any of this. "Your clothes." I shook my head. "Your shoes. No. They haven't changed. They should be worn down to nothing."

He looked away again, out into the blackness down the hall. "Like I said. Lot of possibilities." He cracked a knuckle. "We weren't the only ones who got lost. Bumped into lots of other Nikos and Ryans down here. Most of them dead. Sorry to say." He cracked another knuckle, methodical. "But the clothes are fine, man. The clothes fit great." He forced out a barking laugh, abrupt and cold. I wondered how many years it had taken his laugh to shrivel down to that emaciated sound.

He sniffed. "You get used to it. Stealing clothes, I mean. Stops being strange after a while."

"But how do you eat?" I felt angry, not the least because my skin was crawling at the thought of him grave-robbing other Nikos. Other Ryans. "If you've been down here so long, how the hell are you even alive?"

He turned back to me again, no longer wistful but with a dangerous sharpness. Maybe you've heard the phrase "thousand-yard stare" and maybe you've even seen one before, but I hadn't. It *struck* me. I believed everything he said next, no matter how fantastic. The words were only flavoring on the truth in that stare.

"There's a room," he began, voice graveling, "not much farther down from here. Different from anything up here. Bigger. A bit bigger." That laugh again. "Can't walk the length of one of its walls without stopping to sleep. Takes five or six sleeps to walk all the way around, keeping the outer wall to your left the whole time. Passing all the doors." He shook his head. "Maybe a few thousand halls leading out. Most of them slanting upward. But only one goes back to the surface. The rest lead nowhere, or in circles, back to one of the other ten thousand halls.

He took a breath. "When you come into this room, though, you can tell something's different. The carpet ends. It turns to asphalt."

He stood up so quick I cringed back, but turned to the wall and placed a hand on it. He drew his finger down, then over and around, drawing an invisible square; then drew invisible grid lines in it. "Asphalt," he said. "City streets. City blocks. A huge grid of them. Suburban streets. Crosswalks, stop signs, you know. What you'd expect. Lawns, but they're all dead. No sun, right?"

He turned back, leaned against the wall. "And all the houses," he said, fixing me with that stare again, "are ours."

"What?" I couldn't break his gaze.

He shrugged. "Not exactly. None exactly. But all close enough. Sometimes the foyer's a mirror image, or the front door's changed, or there's one more bedroom on the second floor, one less. Or the carpet's different, or the wallpaper, or the kitchen's smaller or there's no bricked up fireplace, or the fireplace is bigger, or there's a fish tank instead of a fireplace. Sometimes, maybe one in ten houses, I can't see a difference. But I think it's always there. Not that I've checked them all." He laughed again. "Did the math once. There's ten million houses. Give or take. I've been down here a long time. But not that long.

"Each one has that upstairs porch room, though," he went on, relentless. "Your room. And they're all filled with your stuff. Little variations again. Sometimes your bookshelf has a copy of *Dhalgren*, sometimes it doesn't. That one I always look for. But it's your room, in every house. And your bed.

"And under every one of those beds, there's another Down-stairs, as big as this one. And if you can find your way down, another huge empty city with another ten million houses. Each slightly different. Each slightly different than the ten million up here. And sometimes, other Ryans and Nikos come up out of them, expecting to find the real world, with people and a sun and all. They're real fucking disappointed. Especially when they wander too far and can't find the house they came out of again.

"Sometimes I'll meet them on the streets, crying, panicked. I stay away, of course. Can't get too close, like you know, or. Bad things happen." He pointed to his temples, and I flashed back to that feeling of wrongness when my double and I had almost bumped into each other.

He looked away. "Course they're usually dead by the time I find them," he added lightly. "But. Your question. Each house has a pantry, food. Once in a while one has power, too, lit up like Christmas in all that dark, and the fridge is running and cold, and there's lunchmeat and milk and leftovers inside. Unspoiled. So there's plenty to eat. Just not a lot of, you know. Ambiance."

He stepped closer. "I heard your gunshots. That's how I found you. Don't know what you were shooting at but doesn't matter. *You're not lost.* Are you." He glanced behind me, back the way I'd come. "This goes back up, doesn't it? To the surface. The real surface." He closed his eyes. "With light and birds, and grass, and people who aren't you or me. I can't tell you..." He opened them again and I wanted to shrink back, close my eyes and pretend I'd never seen something like that in human eyes, let alone in his, that hollowness and greed and something else, too, something worse. But I couldn't. I could only stare back, cringing.

"I can't tell you," he said more quietly, "what it would mean to me to find my way back up there. Orion. I can't stay down here any longer. I can't."

$$\geqslant 12 \leqslant$$

I wanted to find my Niko, but this one kept arguing against it. Impossible, he said. Like finding a needle in a haystack. Except this haystack went down forever. In the best-case scenario, he explained patiently, we'd wander until our food ran out, and then with our last dregs of energy and luck find our way back up to the surface and out, empty-handed.

He didn't mention the worst-case scenario.

Pacing up and down up a hallway anchored only by the orange beacon of the glowstick, we argued. He insisted the smartest strategy was for us to retrace my steps to the base of the slide and climb back up. "The closer to the top, the fewer possibilities," he said, "the fewer choices. And fewer chances of making the wrong one." When he found out I hadn't seen my Niko since we got separated in the shaft, he grew even more convinced. "Maybe he's not down here at all. Maybe he caught himself on the way down, like you said, and he's up there now waiting for you. Worrying." He gave up convincing me. "Or if he's not, he'll realize heading back is the smart option. I *know* he would, buddy." He tapped his head. "Trust me."

I couldn't deny this plan made sense, but I felt sick. Too much was wrong. "Look. Even if I take you back up there, it won't be your world. You can't stay. If you're on the wrong side too long, you start to feel—detached." I shuddered without meaning to. "Like it's rejecting you. Like antibodies swarming. It'll kill you."

He shrugged. "You don't know that. I'll risk it. Anything's better than staying down here."

"It's not just that." I felt like a coward, but desperately wanted an excuse, a reason he couldn't come back with us. "You know about that sick feeling when you're too close to a twin. That's even worse than the headaches. So say we find my Niko and get you both back to the surface. Then what? The two of you get a double on campus, move in together?"

He sighed, impatient. "You think I haven't thought this through, all the time I've had? You help me get back up, I'm gone. It's a big planet. I've learned how to survive. I'll never get within a hundred miles of either of you again."

"Wait a minute." I'd had an idea. "That sick sensation, when you're too close. We can use that to find him." He raised an eyebrow. "Okay, maybe you're right, and there's too much space here to find him by dumb luck. But you've got a sixth sense for where he is. You're like a magnet we can move through that haystack, feeling for tugs. Any twinges and we steer closer, till we're close enough to do the rest by shouting."

"You're not listening to me, Orion." He was getting angry. He realized it, took a moment to collect himself. "There's a lot of space down here. You have no idea how much space. You're never going to find him. You need to accept that. You'll get us both lost. And I'm *sick* of being lost, buddy. Fucking sick of it."

He had an intensity my Niko never had—though maybe there'd been something like it latent in him, waiting for the right trauma to pull it out like a loose thread. It scared me.

He was right. I didn't want to get lost down here, either. I didn't want to end up like him.

But I also wasn't willing to give up on my Niko.

I dug out my keys, held them up. "Look. I've been using these to mark my way. There's no chance of getting lost. And I've got plenty of food, still. For both of us. So we keep searching. Keep marking the way. Be methodical, map it out. And if the food runs low..." My throat felt tight. "If that happens, we'll turn back. But I can't give up on him yet. I can't."

His eyes narrowed, and I could see him weighing something behind them. But then his face relaxed. A huge smile broke across it, and it was so familiar, so him, that when he threw his arms around me and squeezed me tight, I hugged him back.

"Goddammit, man, you haven't changed at all. Okay." He pulled back, still grinning, and laughed—a real laugh, the one I remembered. "Shit. Like you'd give me up without a fight. Course not. The fuck we waiting for, then?"

He hoisted his pack, started down the hall. "Come on, Ry," he shouted back over his shoulder, "let's go find me."

Elder Niko was obsessive about marking our way—I couldn't blame him—so we made slow progress. But despite his initial misgivings he seemed committed now to finding his younger double. Even downright cheerful about it.

We slipped into something like a rhythm, despite the surreal circumstances. He declined my offer of a glowstick, and didn't pull out the penlight or whatever from his shirt pocket, instead keeping close to me as I swung my light around, peering down all the hallways we passed. Sometimes, for a moment, I'd forget it wasn't him. Then the light would catch the hard-edged crow's feet around his eyes, or he'd ask in nostalgia-tinged tones if I remembered something that happened a week or a month ago, and reality crashed back into me. I supposed from his perspective I was like a long-lost friend at a high school reunion, so as woozy as it made me feel I could understand this behavior.

I thought I could, anyway.

He didn't seem to need much light. I asked about this and he shrugged, saying he spent most of his time in total darkness. Sometimes, he said, there were long stretches between lit-up rooms, between scavenged batteries or glowsticks. My skin crawled when I imagined trying to navigate this endless labyrinth by feel, never knowing when you might step into a puddle of water, a bottomless shaft. A body. I thought of him wandering these halls in utter darkness, face placid, eyes unfocused, fingers skimming the paneled wall, the only sound the scuff of sneakers on carpet. Sniffing for rot at hallway junctions. Feeling on hands and knees for corpses and their backpacks of supplies, like a blind crab scavenging for leavings at the bottom of the sea. I thought of getting so used to this that it no longer seemed awful. That it seemed perfectly normal.

The sense that he was keeping something from me, that something was wrong, only grew. He kept asking about the way back up: casually, like making conversation. But he wanted to know what was above the slide, whether we'd come through a fridge or a sliding glass door, whether the junction before the long stairs down had eight doors or six or five, whether we'd found the Library Chasm, which branch I'd taken off the Big Room to get down here. He was trying to reconstruct the route back out. Maybe this made sense—maybe he was just curious, or hedging his bets in case we got split up, like I had with my Niko—but behind the jokes and easy laughter I sensed calculation. A front. Performance.

Now and then I'd ask if he'd gotten any twinges of feeling, hints we were getting close to another Niko. He'd answer right away: Nope. Nothing. Sorry. At one point, annoyed, I demanded he stop for a minute and really try. He apologized with abashed sincerity, and we stood at a junction for ten long minutes while he concentrated, the wrinkles around his eyes creasing as he squeezed them closed—but when he opened them again, he shook his head. Nothing. He seemed sad but not surprised.

Like he already knew there was no one to find.

We'd come to a place of endless ducts and exposed plumbing. Bulky metal curves and protrusions poked from the walls: the bones of water heaters, of central air. The ground was dry, but the room felt hot and moist, dripping all around us. We poked around a space the size of a mansion, cluttered with oddly-sized corners and crannies, finally realizing the whole area was a dead end. There was no other way out.

"Maybe it's time to turn back," Elder Niko said when we realized this, solemn. We were near the back of the big cluttered space. A smell like rotting leaves wafted from the sharp metal ruins of a boiler that looked like it had ruptured from the inside. The carpet was mottled with rusty blotches, like overlapping pools of dried-up blood. "Man, it's going to be hilarious when we find out my younger self's been topside this whole time. Lounging on a blanket in the backyard, you know, under the sky. Catching some rays. Waiting for you to get out." He laughed, and his voice echoed off a thousand metal boxes.

His face grew more serious. "Or maybe he's so lost we'll never find him. Orion. I tried to tell you. This place is too big." He gestured around us, took a deep breath, looked chagrined. "It's a lost cause, buddy. I think it's time to give it up."

He took a step toward the door, but I was in his way, bristling. Holding my ground.

He stopped, looking confused. "What's up?"

I couldn't explain my trembling, except for a deep-seated certainty that this was wrong. Everything about it was wrong, just generally, but a specific wrong thing was the way this place had taken Niko from me and done this to him, made him into something I couldn't understand and didn't trust, and I couldn't stand this stalemate any more. Some yawning possibility loomed before me, like I was blindfolded on a precipice, about to step forward. But I had to know. Better to fall than keeping lingering on the edge.

I met his eyes. "Tell me."

"Hmm?"

"Tell me whatever you're not telling me. What's really going on. I want to know."

He frowned. "What do you mean?"

"Damn it, stop *pretending*. Everything is not okay. You're stringing me along and you need to stop it. Be honest with me."

"Oh?" His expression had started to shift. Something was slipping.

"Stop playing games." I clenched my fists. "Stop *using* me. Look, we can do this together. You need me to get out of here. Both of you do. I know the way back, and I'll help you, but I need to trust you. And you need to trust me. Okay?"

He nodded, looking serious, and bowed his head. Then gave himself one final nod. As if coming to a decision.

He looked up smiling, stepped forward, and punched me in the throat.

I staggered back, pain exploding from my neck, but he stepped forward at the same time, looking bored. He punched me in the face so hard I spun sideways and slammed into the wall, something crunching in my nose, and he kept stepping forward, grabbing my wrists and kicking my feet out from under me. He twisted my arms as I fell so I landed face first, and still he kept moving with me, descending with his knee in my back so when I hit the ground his full weight slammed down on top of me. He punched me hard in the kidney, twice, grinding my face into the carpet with his other hand now somehow on my head.

My mouth was open but I couldn't breathe, or scream or speak or think for lack of breathing. My throat felt crushed, my lungs paralyzed. Pain like a stab wound tore open my side. I couldn't think enough to move my muscles.

Never taking his weight off the knee digging into my spine, he pulled something from his bag. I heard a rip, and was so sure it was some part of myself it confused me when I felt no pain. Something sticky wrapped around my wrists, tugging at the hairs on my forearm. Duct tape. And now I did struggle, feebly trying to dislodge him, kicking my legs. Pathetic as a half-squashed bug, twitching, not realizing it's already dead. In moments he'd bound my ankles, too, and then my knees.

It had all taken maybe ten seconds.

I tried to make a sound, to beg him to stop, or ask why he was doing this, but all that came out was a coarse rasp, not even a gasp. So I begged with my eyes instead.

He met them and laughed. He knew what I was trying to say. It amused him.

He frisked me: hands patting my ass, my pockets, my crotch. "Gun," he said, impatient, "where's the gun?"

I had just enough breath back to grunt a word. "Lost."

"Stupid." He cuffed the back of my head. "There's worse things than me down here. And worse *me*s." He smirked, but his hands had found my back pocket, felt what was inside. They reached in, urgent, and dragged out the key. His breath caught.

He bent down and shoved it in my face, angrier now than he'd looked while beating the shit out of me. "What's this? How long ago did you find this?"

My head spun, trying to think of some way to regain control. "Couple," I gasped. "Hours."

"Have you used it yet? Gone through?"

I didn't want to answer his questions, but I couldn't see how lying would help me, either. I shook my head.

He stood up and punched the wall, leaving his fist in the cracked indentation it made for a long moment. Then he started to pace, furious. Thinking. I groaned and rolled partway onto my side. The pain in my kidney was evolving from a stabbing into a roiling burning sickness, like something inside me boiled, threatened to burst. Breathing felt like forcing air through pipes sealed with rust.

"My Niko," I rasped. "Looking for me. Won't let you. Do this."

"Your Niko's dead," he said, and he said it so simply, so matter-of-fact, it sunk into me like another punch. "Found him and got rid of him before I found you. I always kill the Nikos first. Makes the headaches go away faster."

It felt like the room was dropping. I didn't want to believe him. I fought not to. "No," I gasped. "Bull. Shit."

He reached into his shirt pocket and pulled out what I'd thought was a penlight. It wasn't. It was a finger.

He tossed it onto the carpet by my face and it rolled once, coming stiffly to rest a few inches from my eye. It was cut through at the knuckle and pale and dead. But more or less the right color.

"I've killed him hundreds of times," he said, sounding bored again. He was watching me, though, and as he noticed my tears he gave them a small, sad smile, as if touched by my naiveté. "And you, too, you little bitch. You're even easier. Always freeze up at first. Or if you don't, you try to grab my arm. But the same way every time, right? So that makes it simple to break your wrist. When you double over whining, it's easy to grab your skull and smash it into the ground until you stop moving."

He knelt down, turning his head sideways to study my face, as if curious about the effect his words were having on me. "This time's different, though. *You're* not lost yet. *You* know the way back." He reached out and tousled my hair, playful-rough. "And you're going to take me there, Orion. Take me back up. Or you're going to die."

He stood up again. "But this fucking key. Complicates things. You said you're on the wrong side, from your perspective. Yeah?" I didn't answer; he went on as if I had. "That means there's another you who's also found a key. The twin key to this one, on the twin side. And if that other you didn't get ambushed by his old bestie"—a wicked grin—"he'll pop through to this side soon enough. Because. You find a key, you're almost certainly only a few hours away from finding its door."

I couldn't see how this changed things. "Why does that m-matter?"

He turned the key over and over in his hand, staring at it. "Staying in sync. Wasn't that always our theory? I think we have to. Buddy. I told a lie earlier. I don't always kill you both right away. Sometimes I... ask questions." He scraped a thumbnail along the key. "Find out where you've been. What happened before. The ones who have it worst are always the ones who got too out of sync. With their doubles. There's lots of connection points but the higher-up they are, the easier to get—misaligned. Two lasers pointing at each other, yeah? Nudge them just a bit, and instead of meeting, the beams go on forever." I thought of the tunnel with the infinite fridge, and shuddered. "And if two sides lose sync entirely... if things warp too out of true..." He made a sucking sound through his teeth, bringing it to a crescendo and then cutting it off, like a tire popping in reverse.

He glanced at me, then back to the key. "That's what happened to me. My double and I, we... diverged. And something tore. Or popped, maybe. Forget lasers. Think pairs of soap bubbles, floating in infinite void. They need each other to stay stable. Our universes got too far apart and it wasn't good for them. They're gone now, or too far to ever reach. Dark.

"But yours..." He grinned even more broadly. "A ripe pair. Undamaged. Still connected. To each other, and to you. You. I can follow you back into them like a thread. Like a fucking thread, Orion. Up and out and back and into the light."

This is the part where if I was a spy or an action hero, I'd be secretly digging a knife out of my pocket, working my way free of the bonds, taking advantage of the villain's distracted ranting to try for my freedom. But I wasn't a spy. I was a Bio major. I'd never been in a fight. I was trussed up, I couldn't move, the pain was still excruciating, and I had no idea what to do.

As if to reinforce my stupid squandered opportunity, Niko seemed to notice me again. Abruptly he put the key in his pocket (his front right pocket, I noticed, desperate not to be completely helpless) and dug through my pack. With a satisfied grunt, he pulled out rope, and proceeded to tie my hands and lower arms behind my back, so tight my elbows almost touched.

My freedom was slipping away. I tried to keep him talking. "But..." I had to clear my throat, heavy. "If Niko's dead—my Niko—isn't it too late? How can anything be in sync now?"

He paid no attention to this, continuing his rope work. When he was done he wrapped the end a few times around my neck and fear spiked through me, but then he lifted me gently to a sitting position, leaning against the wall.

He went to the pack and pulled out my flashlight, shaking it. "This thing work?" I didn't answer: he was already toggling the switch on and off with no effect. He grunted, dug some batteries from his own pack and slipped them in, nodding in satisfaction as the light came on. Pocketing it, he rummaged through my pack, eyes lighting up when he found my cache of food. He ripped open the wrapper on a power bar and took a huge bite, grunting in satisfaction.

"Niko," I said, trying not to cry. "Please let me go."

He grimaced, like what I'd said had hurt him, and scooted closer to me, still chewing. He ran his fingers gently through my hair, tugged back my head. Stared into my eyes with a frown. Like he'd lost something in them.

"I told another little fib earlier, bud," he said, swallowing. "Sometimes those houses down there do have power, like I said. Who knows why or where it comes from, but sometimes they do."

I kept my eyes on his, hoping to find some empathy or humanity there.

He took another bite. Chewed more slowly this time.

There was nothing in his eyes.

"Power," he said, mouth half-full, "but the fridges and pantries, in all those houses? They're empty. All of them. There's no food down there, Orion. None at all."

I was trembling. I couldn't look away from his eyes.

He swallowed again, shoved the last of the bar into his mouth. Still gripping me with his other hand, he turned my head from side to side, like he was admiring it. "But you and me," he said, mouth full, "other versions. Man, there's *so many* of us. Popping up out of those houses, those millions of houses. Lost. Always lost. Pathetic. Eaten all their food. Starving, out of their minds. They're already dead, really. Or a nudge away."

He swallowed the last of the power bar, licked his lips and the crumbs off his fingers. Then he leaned forward, slow, like he was going in for a kiss.

He stopped, face inches from mine.

"Wouldn't it be such a waste?" His breath smelled of processed figs. "Such a shame for all those deaths to have been for nothing. To have served no purpose. Don't you think?"

"Niko," I begged, wanting it to mean so many things.

His finger touched my lips. "I think you get it. So. We have to find the door this key connects to. We have to wait for your doubles to come through—yours, and your dead friend's. Swap places with them. Pass back to your side. Keep things *synchronous*. And then head up, up, up into the shallows, back to the surface, away from this place forever, and synchronicity can go fuck itself." He stood up, reaching down, and grabbed my shirt to jerk me to my feet. He wrapped the end of the rope around his arm.

"But we'd better get moving. Cause your door's going to be farther down from here. And best for both of us if we find it before I get too fucking hungry." He gestured back toward the way out of the jumbled room of metal tubes, mockingly polite. "After you, amigo."

≫ 13 ≪

Like a bitter parody of the exploring I'd done with my Niko, a million years ago, we kept moving. I led, Niko following behind holding the rope wound around my neck. He'd cut the duct tape from my ankles so I could walk, but tied a blindfold made from a damp shirt tight around my face. "Little handicap," he said, "case you decide to run off." I cringed when he clapped me playfully on the back. "Don't worry, bud. If you're good, I'll tell you when you're about to walk into a pit."

We searched. At intersections he'd describe each hallway, and casually discuss which way to go, as if we were equals. As if he hadn't threatened to kill me and worse. Other than a preference for moving toward anything weird or different, he seemed content to let me choose the direction. He marked the wall, tracing our path with fastidious care—"If we're doing it on this side, they're doing it on theirs, too"—and on the whole seemed downright cheerful. For a while he whistled something I finally placed as the theme to one of our favorite shows. Just the second bar, over and over again.

Like he'd forgotten the rest.

I made little plans for how to get away.

None of them seemed very plausible.

From his descriptions, I gathered we were passing through a maze of identical drab halls. The carpet underfoot was sometimes dry, sometimes thick with something that felt like dead mulch and made me stumble, and often slick with slime and mold. We must have been only just above the water table, if such a concept made sense down here. Probably it didn't. Sometimes we'd go up dry stairs to a soaked hall at the top, or along a downward slant that went from squelchy to dusty. We were near water, anyway, moving through histories of past inundation. Niko described walls streaked with damage from it, paint browned and peeling. Once he found some mushrooms growing from a split baseboard, and stopped to eat them. I could hear him chewing, a slimy sound. The smell as they mixed with his saliva was of pond scum and rotting dirt. He offered me one, but I declined, and he seemed unsurprised. He said they'd keep you alive but weren't especially satisfying. I tried not to hear menace in that.

There were few side rooms here, but he'd open the door to each we passed and check it. Bedroom-sized, he told me, sometimes empty, sometimes filled with chaotic mounds of furniture in broken, ruined pieces. A small drain in the center of each floor, sometimes clogged with sawdust, splinters, and grime, leaving stagnant puddles of mold-choked sludge.

It was hard to keep my balance, blindfolded and with arms bound behind me, and I stumbled a lot. The adrenaline from earlier had worn off, leaving behind a dozen throbbing aches and a deep exhaustion. How long had I been down here? I couldn't come up with a number, but my body knew the answer. Too long.

At the next intersection I tripped on a rough patch of carpet and collapsed, smacking my chin against the ground. It hurt, and I started crying. Sobbing, actually. I'd never felt more useless, pathetic. Niko told me to shut up, and I tried to pull myself together. He sighed, and suggested we take a rest. Sniffling, I agreed.

He sat me up against a wall. I clenched and unclenched my tingling hands; from the elbows down everything was numb. After a while the tears stopped.

I wanted to sleep but couldn't bear waking back up to this. I wanted him to untie me, unwind the rope from my neck, let me go. I wanted to get away from him, or better yet for none of this to ever have happened at all. I wanted to be dreaming of something other than hallways, and him.

I could have none of these things. But he hadn't gagged me. I could still talk. And maybe talking together, like we'd done so much, I could find a way to reach him.

So I asked him about the things he'd seen, and he told me.

He spoke of a room whose floor was a chaos of school desks, plastic bucket seats and flip-down wooden tops. How he'd excavated them out at least ten feet deep without seeing signs of a floor. He spoke of corridors whose floors and ceilings began to steepen in either direction, rising up to the vertical, gigantic carpeted wheels serving no rational purpose.

He spoke of more connection points between paired dimensions, useless to him since he couldn't find his way to the surface of any—and all *tangled* down there, he said again. The connections always had some kind of airtight seal. Steam-filled wood saunas with a door at each end; school lockers just big enough to stand in with doors on each end; a shower, but vertically stretched, thirty feet of bathroom tile with frosted glass doors at the top and bottom, and climbing its steel fixtures, faucets and knobs sticking out at random from the walls, climbing it all the way to the top.

He spoke of curving tunnels made from scraps of sandpaper and carpet samples, of flooded libraries swimming with illegible books, of a maze of closet the size of a city block, endless cramped turns ducking under dusty coat hangers. A maze of crawlways through half-sized doors, like the ones you see opening onto water heaters or the electric meter, that he'd gotten lost in for a week. He spoke of vast caves made entirely of stairs: walls, floor and ceiling expanding and contracting in carpeted, ninety-degree edges. Of pits with barely-heard voices rising from their invisible depths, and the things the voices said if you listened long enough.

Finally, he trailed off, and we steeped together for a while in the thick, unbroken quiet. I was trying to think what I could say to keep him talking, but he broke the silence first.

"You would have gone wild for some of that shit, man. Wish you could have been there." His voice was wistful. "All our crazy, stupid theories. We were wrong about everything. But it was more fun being wrong together."

I licked my lips. Maybe this was my chance.

"Yeah. Hell yeah," I started. "Jesus, man, I can't imagine what it's been like for you." *Isn't the phrase "I can only imagine?"* some part of my brain whispered. I shook it off. "I mean, I don't know what I'd have done, if it were me. Alone down here." I took a breath, extemporizing. "You've... done things to survive, and I mean who could blame you? Who's to say when push comes to shove what's right or wrong when survival's at stake?"

He didn't make a sound, and I couldn't see his face through the blindfold. But I sensed a tide shifting. I'd said something wrong. My chance was slipping away.

"*You don't have to do this to me.*" I hadn't meant to say it and not with such pitiful desperation, but now I couldn't help myself, couldn't stop babbling. "We're friends. You're my friend. We're only going to survive by working together. You don't have to keep me tied up like this. I want the same thing you want. To get out, get the fuck out of here—"

"Friends." he interrupted, voice dangerously quiet. "Is that what we were? Back in the day?"

My chest was tight. "Weren't we?"

I heard a scratching sound. A dog itching itself. I couldn't see but had a clear image: he was scratching the hair behind his ear, head tilted, half-turned down. Something he always did right before explaining something he didn't think he should have to explain.

"I've had a lot of time to think, Ry." His voice was still calm.

"About our *friendship*. About *us*." I jerked: he'd rested his fist on the top of my shoe. "Why we ended up down here."

I was losing him, or had already lost him, but I didn't know how or why or what I could say to reverse it. "Yeah?"

"Yeah," he said, lifting the fist and letting it fall back on my sneaker. "I think maybe there was more going on than I really appreciated at the time. For. Example." He punctuated each word with a harder bap on my foot. "We only found this place because of you. Remember? Because you found it, underneath your bed."

"Okay," I said, "but—"

He shushed me, and I sensed him stiffen, twist his head away. He switched on the flashlight and dim light filtered through the blindfold. He seemed to be pointing it down the hallway, back the way we had come.

"What is it?"

"Shut up. Did you hear anything?"

I shook my head, vague distant relief mingling with fresher fear. "No."

Silence. It seemed to expand in my head, like those disposable earplugs, eating up all the empty space.

Finally he turned back toward me. "I think something's following us."

Some*thing*. Not someone. Oh. "Like what?"

"You know about the other versions of us down here." He snickered. "More than you'd like to. The doubles, and their doubles from the other houses, and so on. They're us, more or less exactly. Which is why we get that sick feeling when they're close. And because they're us exactly, it makes them easy to take out. Don't have to learn their weaknesses, because fuck, you already know them." He paused for a moment. "But there's... other ones."

I wasn't sure I wanted to prod, but found myself doing it anyway. "Other ones?"

He shook his head. "Ever see someone watching you down

here? Like at the edge of your light?"

"No," I said, hair rising. "I mean... I don't think so."

"If you get closer, you can see they look like us, too. Always a Niko or an Orion. On the outside, anyway." The pattern of light shifted as he swung it down each of the other hallways, then back to the first again. "When you get close to a double of yourself, you can feel it. Right? Feels wrong, somehow. Bad. Something to do with the synchronicity, I think, the risk. If the two of you see each other get out of sync, if you understand you've broken it... bad news, and your body senses it. That danger.

"But. These other things. You get close to one of them, even if it looks like you, you don't feel anything at all. And that somehow makes it so much worse." He spat. "Because it means the Semblances aren't human. They look like us, but they're not, not really. They're something else."

"You named them the fucking Semblances?" I was horrified. "Thanks. Not creepy at all."

He laughed a genuine laugh, then cut it short, like he was upset with himself. Like I was pulling something over on him. "They *are* creepy, dumbshit. They just stand there. They don't usually come too close, but if you walk up to them, they don't move away. They don't move at all. They watch you." He sniffed. "I mean they move their eyes, you know. To track you. Their heads. They breathe." He unscrewed the water bottle and took a swig. "But they don't respond to anything you do. *Anything.*"

He paused, as if to let that sink in. Or as if remembering something.

"And if you walk off," he continued, "they'll follow you. At a distance. But if you stay in one place for too long, sometimes. Sometimes. They kind of creep up on you. Slow. Edge a tiny bit forward every now and then. Like they're eager, but also real, real patient. I woke up one time and two of them, two Nikos, were bent over me. Standing there for fuck knows how long while I slept. Staring. Mona Lisa smiles."

He shrugged. "If you sprint for a while, take some twists and turns, you can shake them. Creepy, yeah, but not a problem."

Oh well that's fine then. "What are they?"

"No idea." He laughed that hollow bark-laugh again. "Maybe echoes, or waves, or something. Waves and particles. Super-impositions. This whole place, Downstairs, it's like some kind of huge multiplier. You've figured that out, right? At least that much? It multiplies. Dimensions, people. Rooms. Ideas. Emotions. Some kind of chain reaction that got started somehow, sometime. There's a spring down here," and he was almost chanting now, murmuring, his voice gone strange, "clear waters at the source. Deep. All the water comes from there. Very, very deep. It splits, and splits, and splits again, and keeps splitting. Thousands of times. Millions. And each stream is as big as the one it's splitting from, and they shouldn't all fit but they do, and it's wrong, it can't fit in your head, it's too big *it's too big...*"

He seemed to catch himself, stiffened.

"But the Semblances," he said, in control again. "They do it too, sometimes. There'll be two of them, moving almost in sync. Or four. I think if two bump into each other, they sort of stick together, cluster up. And if those two meet others, they all join up, like a fucking molecule. Snarled in bigger and bigger tangles." He was watching me now, I guessed; I got the sense he was smirking, enjoying the effect the story was having on me. "One time I had to walk through a whole room full of them. All just standing there, packed shoulder to shoulder as I shoved my way through. They weren't doing anything. Just looking. Looking at me."

I turned my head nervously in the direction of the hallway I couldn't see. "And you think there's one back there now?"

"Oh, I know there is," he said. "It's standing right there, watching you."

I jolted back, lost my balance, and topped over, kicking back with my feet and scrambling to right myself. My skin was crawling and all I wanted was to get farther away, except I couldn't see it, couldn't see anything, and *what if a second one is coming up behind me—*

But Niko was laughing now, and it slowly dawned on me through my terror what that probably meant.

"You fucking pussy." He climbed to his feet, grunting. "Dumb of me. If you'd wet your pants I'd have to smell it the rest of the way."

I awkwardly struggled upright, stood, furious. He made no move to help.

But I knew him too well. He might have been bluffing at the end, but only to cover for being legitimately scared. He *had* heard something down the hall, or thought he had. And he hadn't been teasing when he'd started talking.

At least some of that had been true.

He tugged on the rope around my neck. "Storytime's over, bitch. Get moving."

Walking blind into the unknown isn't fun, and gets worse when you're freshly terrified of it. I kept expecting now to walk into a body, someone standing in my way, fleshy and warm and inhuman. Staring. But I didn't. To my captor's credit, he never let me walk into a wall (or a pit), although he was sometimes rough with jerks to the rope around my neck to correct me.

But I was reaching the limits of my endurance. My collapse by the nightlight felt like eons ago, and maybe I'd only slept for an hour or two there, anyway. Waves of emotion had washed through me since then, each one leaving its own high-water mark. I stumbled even over level ground. I was barely awake.

Niko finally noticed, and agreed we could stop for "a sleep." He let me lie down, but kept my head covered and hands tied. It was better than nothing.

It's a testament to the depth of my exhaustion that I fell asleep within moments. This time, I didn't dream.

I blinked awake some time later, not quite sure what had woken me. Niko breathed quietly, a few feet away. I got the sense he was sitting up against the wall, legs folded up, and I was lying at his feet in the center of the hall. It was dark. He must have turned the flashlight off, not that I'd be able to see much anyway with a t-shirt tied around my face.

I wondered if I could, very slowly and quietly, wriggle away. Like a worm out of a tackle box.

He reached out and nudged me with his foot. "Don't even think about it, bitch." But the nudge was gentle, and his voice tired.

We stayed there for a long moment, listening to each other breathe.

Finally, he exhaled, loud, frustrated. "You think I want this?" He sounded desperate. Near tears. "I don't. Any of it. Scaring you like this. I'm not a monster, man, I don't get off on it. I'm doing what I have to. You don't get that, I know, but you haven't been down here long enough. Nowhere near long enough."

I stayed quiet, afraid to say something that might make him angry again.

He sighed. "I don't always kill you, either. Or at least not right away. Sometimes, first. For old times' sake, you know. I fuck you."

The word *fuck* stung me.

He leaned forward, holding his head a foot above mine. His breath tickled the fabric at my ear. "You do remember, don't you? The time we did it?" He sounded concerned. "That night, after I tried to kill myself?"

Sometimes when a person is stung their body overreacts. They swell up, maybe so much their eyes are forced shut. It's called anaphylaxis. Unprotected, in the Greek. But the point is it's not the sting that's doing it to you, not really. It's your own body, blinding you and destroying itself in a misguided attempt to keep you safe.

"Yes," I whispered.

"That was maybe the closest I ever felt to anyone." His voice was calm, bland, like recounting a decent lunch he'd had. "I loved you so much. Not in that way, you know. Not the way you wanted me to. But I figured what the fuck. You saved me. No, not just that." His finger brushed my cheek through the fabric and I flinched. "You *needed* me. I was *everything* to you. That felt so fucking good."

I was trying to stay motionless. I remembered a safety video they'd made us watch at Yellowstone. *If you're on the ground and a bear attacks you, curl into a ball and play dead. Don't fight back. The bear will win.*

I couldn't open my eyes, couldn't breathe. Maybe it was the anaphylaxis. Something somewhere was terrifying. Doppelgangers lurking in basement hallways. A camper in a tent, terrified by his own snores.

The bear will win.

His hand moved over the shirt wrapped around my head, not quite touching it, not quite pulling away. "I want to get that feeling back sometimes, you know? It's so fucking lonely here. You can't blame me." He laughed, so loud and close to my face I cringed. "I mean. Don't get me wrong. I'd prefer a girl but there aren't any down here. Just us. Only us."

His fingers outlined my face. "Anyway. Doesn't work. Never works. Never the same with you." He breathed out through his nostrils and it tickled the fabric by my cheek. "I can't trust you. Any of these versions of you. Ry, Ryan, Orion. You seem different but you're all the same. Everything you ever said or did after that. Was bullshit. None of you gave a shit about me, did you? What I needed. Who I was. You just wanted it to happen again.

"And the next time I tried to off myself, that's the only reason you stopped me, isn't it?" He rapped his knuckles on my forehead, through the shirt. "Isn't it, bitch."

"No." It was so soft, I'm not even sure he heard me.

I could feel him shrug. "Anyway, that's why I kill you, after. Case you were wondering."

He sat back up, wincing. "But sorry, man, not tonight. Got a headache." He stood, kicked me in the side. "Come on. Better keep moving. We're close. I can feel it."

≫ 14 ≪

Before long the floor began to change. First it went glossy-smooth, then to shag, then to changing patterns and textures of creaking wood, tile, and carpet. I stumbled more and more over bumps and irregularities, as if the floor was crumpling, bunching up as we neared some pressure point.

Niko opened every door we passed now. At the third one after we slowed down, he sucked in a sharp breath.

"Definitely on the right track. You're gonna need eyes for this, kiddo." He pulled my blindfold free.

I blinked in the sudden glare from his light. He stood between me and the open doorway at the end of the hall. It was dark inside, though I could see something glittering in the gloom behind him. Ice?

"Take a look," he said with a grin. "I'll shine the light. But don't lean too far in. I wouldn't bet your life on my grip on the rope."

Wondering what he meant, I shuffled to the doorframe. He turned and shined the light past me, and that's when the vertigo hit.

The door opened onto nothing. Past the frame, the floor dropped away into blackness. The flashlight only went so far, of course, so I shouldn't have been able to tell how far down the drop-off went.

Except I could.

Far, far below us were tiny clusters of lights. Irregularly spaced, but stretching out in all directions. Maybe miles down. It was like the view out the window of a red-eye, flying over suburbia at night.

That wasn't what gave me the vertigo.

Curving down from the base of the doorway was a filigreed structure I couldn't at first identify. My impression of ice was wrong: it was laid out more like a spiderweb, a grid of sparkly intersecting lines. As I squinted I realized the sparkles were countless tiny crystals, dangling from some kind of mesh and reflecting back the flashlight in hundreds of shimmering glints. As the web curved down and away it grew denser and denser, strands converging towards a point maybe sixty feet below and another sixty away from the door. The lines of dangling crystal converged there into an dense, scintillating object a couple feet across.

A chandelier. I blinked. It hung with no obvious point of support above a long narrow platform covered in junk. It was as if the chandelier had exploded, but only in one direction, toward us: crystals multiplying and propagating outward and upward in an ever-widening wave of fractal repetition, connecting the chandelier to our hallway with a web of glass.

"It's a Confusion," Niko said with a satisfied grin. "Means we're real close now."

"A what?" I backed away from the horrifying drop-off.

"What I call them." He shrugged. "Most of Downstairs tends to follow normal architectural rules. Walls, floor, ceiling, measurements more or less what you'd expect. Bedroom objects in bedrooms." He played his light along the chandelier-net, watching its cut-glass facets sparkle. "But close to a connection point, things get jumbled up. Like it's harder to maintain the semblance of order, for some reason."

I thought of our fridge, in a kitchen with a pool that had a door at the bottom.

"This one," he added, frowning down, "is pretty fucking weird, though."

Still struggling with vertigo (tipping forward, arms bound, unable to stop myself as I crashed through the flimsy web and tumbled into blackness) I followed his gaze. The lines of chandelier-stuff converged above what I'd at first seen as a narrow strip of ground some way below and in front of us, itself suspended over that awful drop. But as I focused on the strip of ground, I realized it wasn't a flat surface, but something more complex: a sort of huge tube or pipe, maybe thirty feet thick, stretching away in both directions. It made slow, lazy curves as it went, like an immense statue of a snake slithering through grass. You could walk flat along the top of the snake's back in either direction, assuming you could get down there in the first place. Its endpoints, if any, were lost in darkness.

And it got weirder.

The tube appeared to be made of the same scuffed, dusty hardwood floor tiles as my bedroom. A profusion of tatty throw rugs clung flat to its surface even on the curving sides, like stickers on a tipped-over water bottle. And a motley collection of bedroom furniture was scattered all around it, also attached in some gravity-defying way to the curved surface. No matter the angle, the furniture rose from the hardwood tube as if down was towards its center. A dresser canted at a forty-five degree angle; the top of a bookshelf poked up around the edge of the curve, like peering over the horizon of a tiny planet. So yeah, picture looking down at a giant snake that had somehow coated itself in superglue and slithered through a secondhand furniture store, encrusting itself with beds, nightstands, dressers, floor lamps (some lit), bookshelves, bureaus, trashcans, and laundry hampers. Escher's own frat house. And all suspended over a miles-high drop down to god knows where, connected to us via exploded rays of chandelier.

"Holy shit," I said.

He laughed. "Damn straight. Okay then. Who wants to go first?"

It was me. Surprise. Niko realized he'd have to untie my hands for me to climb down, and if he went first, there'd be nothing to stop me running off back the way we'd come. I'd be running in the wrong direction, away from the supposed portal back to my own side, but I felt like that might be preferable to being the prisoner of a hungry psychopath who looked like a strung-out version of my dead best friend. Or whatever we were to each other.

Of course, if I went first there'd be nothing to stop me running off along the impossible bedroom-tube, either. Except I'd have exactly two directions to choose from and Niko would have a birds-eye view on which one I picked. Academic, anyway: he retied the rope around my ankle, let out enough slack for me to get down, and wound the other end around the doorknob of the last room back, a few paces up the hall.

"This probably won't hold your weight," he added, tugging the rope experimentally. "Not for long anyway. But if I brace myself and take some of the load, it should be enough."

He explained the plan while sliding fresh batteries into a headlamp and tightening it onto my head: I would climb down the chandelier net while he and the doorknob stood ready to catch me if I fell. When I got to the top of the tube-path—the back of the snake—he'd retie the rope to himself, and follow me down while I braced from below. He reminded me that since we'd be tied together, catching him if he fell would be in our mutual interest.

He also mentioned, quite casually, that he had no plans to kill me. Our deal held. Once I got him to the surface, he'd vanish and I'd never see him again. If I messed with him, though— tried to untie my rope while down there and run off, or got funny ideas about yanking it—he would hunt me down. He told me of his expertise at hunting me down—me, personally. He'd done it dozens of times. He'd know which way I'd choose at intersections. Where I'd try to hide.

And once he found me, he'd hurt me. He'd spend a long time hurting me.

He was an expert at that too, he said.

As if to illustrate this point he pulled out a camping knife with a long, serrated blade and flipped it open: the kind you'd use to saw through small deadwood to make tinder. We'd looked at one just like it at the sporting goods store, my Niko and I, but decided not to get it. After admiring it for a moment, he closed it and attached it to his belt. I wondered if this was less a threat than insurance against being tied together above a gut-clenching drop. Maybe some of each.

He watched me watching the knife, with cut-glass intensity.

"Time to go," he said.

I clutched the doorjamb, trying not to stare down at the twinkling lights far below. Trying to think of some way to get out of this.

"What do you think's down there?" I asked, buying time.

He didn't look up, focused on a knot. "I think we're above the City. With all the houses, like I told you. From down there you sometimes see clusters of lights, way up above. This must be one of them."

He pulled the cinch tight. "Rules of geometry don't really make sense this deep, though. Maybe we're already below the City. Maybe this goes down forever."

He got to his feet, wincing and putting a hand momentarily to his temples. "Okay, quit stalling. Get moving."

"Hang on." Fear sweated out of me. "We don't even know if this mesh or net or whatever will hold my weight. Or if this portal you're looking for is even down there."

"It's down there." He set his grip on the rope. "I'm sure of that. But as for your first concern..."

He shrugged, then shoved me, hard.

I flailed, but my body was already past the edge of the door, my hands too slow to grab the frame, world tilting at a sickening angle. My sneaker tried to glue itself to the carpet of the hall but my center of mass was too far out, way too far. My head dropped below my feet and I opened my mouth to scream as I began to fall into nothingness.

With a tinkling smash, I crashed into the net of chandelier. It was like landing on an uncomfortably studded trampoline, sloped sharply down. For a second everything swayed, nauseating, and I scrambled for a grip, but I was slipping, sliding over the scraping glass baubles, down and sideways towards the edge...

With a whimper I clutched the mesh beneath me, wrapping my hands around faceted glass and wire and jamming my feet into gaps. One leg was dangling out into the yawning void of empty space, but my other three limbs were all caught. I jerked to a stop, gasping, swaying, heart pounding so hard I could barely think, spread-eagled like a fly in a tacky, glittering web.

From somewhere above, Niko laughed. "See!" he called down. "Speculate, theorize all you want. Only way to get answers is to dive in head first. Or butt first, in your case." He let out some slack in the rope. "Now untwist your panties and get climbing."

I wriggled away from the unthinkable drop-off, back toward the center of the jangling net. Moving was awkward: the mesh was a grid of thin metal wire, squares maybe eight or nine inches apart up here, but denser farther down. Little glass baubles dangled from it every few inches, sparkling in the beam of my headlamp. The thing was not comfortable to crawl on, and had enough give that it deformed alarmingly as I shifted my weight. The thin mesh cut into my hands unless I was careful; I'd scraped them both, stopping myself from falling.

I looked back up. There was no wall around the hall we'd come through to get here. It stretched back into empty space beyond the limits of my light, wreathed in billowing pink insulation. Huge lumps swelled from the sides, also swaddled in pink: presumably the last few rooms we'd passed. It looked like a long pink tongue, thick with diseased bumps, that we'd wriggled to the end of and crawled out the tip.

Shuddering, I looked down along the path of books, scouting my route to the relative safety of the impossible bedroom's curving surface. The steep slope of the net up here flattened as it dropped and converged to chandelier. I decided facing the net and right-side up was the safest position to start, like climbing down a ladder. When the thing became more horizontal, I'd have to twist around and crawl, then drop the last few feet to the top of the tube.

It was awkward and slow going, in part because I took significantly more care than I strictly needed. I did not want to trust my life to that murderous asshole and a fucking doorknob.

One handhold and foothold at a time (and ignoring Niko's frequent insults and urgings to hurry the fuck up) I finally made it to the chandelier proper, which I noticed, disconcertingly, wasn't connected to anything at all. Nevertheless, it was rock-solid, anchored with implacable tenacity to its chosen point in space, hovering above the top of the tube beneath, as if hanging from the ceiling of an ordinary room.

Carefully, I pushed my feet over the tinkling edge and dropped the few feet to the curving hardwood beneath me.

I landed hard and dropped into a crouch, adrenaline flaring. While nice to be off the chandelier net, this felt only slightly less precarious. The very top of the huge tube was level enough, but the edges curved down on both sides with alarming speed. The zone where I felt comfortable standing was a rounded summit only five or six feet wide; after that, the slope got steeper and steeper.

Looking down the length of the tube, the flat zone of safety stretched forward like a sinuous path, but in no way a clear one.

To navigate it, you'd have to clamber over beds, edge vertiginously around angled desks. It was as if all the furniture was bolted to that cylindrical floor. Turning toward the sickening curve of the drop-off and seeing the tops of bedroom junk poking up from beyond the horizon a few feet away, I again couldn't shake the sense I was on a tiny planet furnished out of the IKEA catalogue and the dregs of garage sales, albeit one stretched from a sphere into an infinitely long cylinder.

Experimentally, I took a few steps curveward, wondering if gravity somehow worked differently here; but it didn't seem to, at least not for me. The angle felt steep and dangerous. My own "down" was still toward the twinkling lights miles below. Whether the furniture really was bolted to the floor or just obeying its own special rules would have to remain a mystery.

I finally remembered Niko, who'd stopped berating me some time ago, and glanced up to see what he was doing. He wasn't there. I frowned. The rope tied to my ankle curved up to the lip of the hall, tracing the path of the chandelier-net, and vanished inside. I was so far below the hallway now I could only see a few feet of walls and ceiling through its open door. The corridor still seemed lit by the refracted glow of a flashlight, moving around somewhere back there, so I figured he hadn't gone far. Maybe he was untying the rope from the doorknob and tying it to himself, so he could follow me down. But he'd been at it a while.

Shit. This was an opportunity, and I was squandering it. I glanced down at the rope tied to my ankle, but there were multiple knots, some kind of Navy-ass shit, pulled so tight my foot was losing circulation. Sharp. I needed something sharp. I cast around desperately. A few paces from me was a nightstand with drawers, and I yanked one open, hoping for—I don't know. Something. Anything. But there was only junk inside: a few dusty paperclips, a mechanical pencil with a missing eraser. A single red prize ticket from a skeeball alley.

I stared at it, despair creeping over me.

Light played across my face. I started and looked up, guilty. Niko was back, peering down distractedly from the hanging doorway, the rope now tied around his waist. He didn't seem to notice what I was doing. He seemed on edge.

"I think there's one of those fucking Semblances up here," he said. "Way, way back in the hall. At the edge of my light. Doesn't matter. Not going back that way, are we? I'm coming down. Find something to brace yourself on. Brace good and tight," he added, "because if I fall and you're not secure, you're coming with me, baby."

Maybe that would be preferable, the best fate for all concerned.

But maybe he was telling the truth. Maybe he really wasn't planning to kill me. Maybe there was a door up ahead for my key. A way back.

Without Niko?

My survival instinct shoved the thought away, like a drowner pushing their rescuer down into the choking depths, desperate to keep their own head above water.

I looked for a way to brace myself, and that's when I discovered the furniture *was* bolted to the floor. Whether on the top of the curve or sticking horizontally out of its side, it was all attached with thick steel bolts at every contact point to the ground, even the plastic trash cans. None of it budged an inch even when I put my whole back into trying to move it.

"Bracing shouldn't be a problem," I shouted up, but there was no response. I figured he hadn't heard—the empty space around us swallowed up sound, creating a surreal distance to everything, like someone had turned down the volume on reality—but when I looked up to shout, Niko was staring back down the hallway behind him again.

"I think it got closer." He glanced down at me for a moment, face unreadable, then looked back down the hall. "While I wasn't looking. Fucking creepy. In fact..." He trailed off, staring at something I couldn't see. My vantage point only showed a couple feet of ceiling.

"What?" My stomach churned, as if in warning.

He didn't look away from whatever he was staring at.

"It's got something in its hand," he said, quite calmly.

Nausea swept through me, chemical fear. Hairs prickled all over my body.

"It's coming toward me, Ry." He was still calm, still staring down the hall. "I'm starting down in twenty seconds. Tie the rope around something. Fast."

Maybe he was messing with me again. Trying to put the fear of god in me so I'd hurry it up.

Or maybe he wasn't. I knew what his calm tone meant. What he hid behind it. He was fucking terrified.

"I've never seen one move like this," he said, voice still calm. "It's running down the hall towards me, now. Ryan. Hurry."

Something inside me screamed. *He's not lying and something is coming and there's nowhere to run and maybe I should let it get him but I'm tied to him I'm fucking tied—*

I ripped my gaze from the floating hall and cast frantically around the narrow path of safety for something secure, anything heavy. There: a bulky bed with a bookcase headboard filled with books and knick-knacks. I scrambled underneath it, over on top of it, then scrambled underneath the bed and back over the top, pulling the rope tied to my ankle behind.

"Hurry up," he shouted from above, still staring down the hall, and then *I could hear it.* Footsteps, beating against the carpet. Something running down the hallway, running flat out. A manic run. Fast. As fast as it could.

"Ready," I shouted up, not sure which side to root for, not sure of anything but the pulse hammering in my ears.

He nodded once, then pulled his gaze away and swung out over the edge, flipping around to face the net, feet feeling for purchase while he clutched the end of the carpet. Focusing on his hands, not glancing down the hall again, he started down. His descent was much quicker than mine, efficient and smooth. But still not fast enough.

It was coming for him. The footsteps thudded the hall above, creaked loose floorboards. They were close.

"Shit," he said. "Shit shit shit." He was still close to the doorway. Too close.

What is it what does it want why is it running what does it have in its...

With shocking suddenness a hand wrapped itself around the doorframe. It gripped it tight as a body appeared behind it, skidding on the carpet, coming to a halt on the edge of the drop-off. I shivered as I saw it, every part of me shocked into motion like I'd leapt into an ice-cold stream. I wanted to scream but couldn't. My gaze was fixed on the thing in the doorway.

And then I recognized its face.

It was Niko. Young again.

My Niko.

He raised his hand and shot his older clone with my gun.

But even as he did, Elder Niko was throwing himself to the side, scrabbling for purchase on the jangling net (*and it can't be my gun*, I thought distantly, *no more bullets*) and younger Niko changed his aim, steadied himself; but Elder snarled, leapt back up four feet of net in a frantic bound, and wrapped his arms around his double's lower legs, hanging his whole weight on them; and younger Niko's knees buckled and he tumbled forward onto the net with a cry.

Or maybe it was me who cried out, I wasn't sure, and I couldn't breathe, because both Nikos were snarling, scrambling for purchase on each other, on the gun, on the precarious net beneath them as they tumbled down it. They were seconds away from slipping off the side, from plunging into the void of empty space beneath us.

"Look out!" I shrieked, but young Niko had jammed his gun

hand through a gap in the net, jerking them both to a halt. The web of chandelier-stuff bucked and heaved, tinkling like a dump truck full of glass. An eyebolt connecting it to the doorframe wrenched free with a splintering groan. I felt the same crawling horror of watching a spider fight a scrabbling insect, vicious, instinctual. Elder Niko plunged his hand through also to the underside of the net, wrestling for the gun. It went off again with a muffled thump, swallowed up by the void around us. Something zipped past my face in the same instant and I ducked, belatedly, eyes still glued on the fight above.

Elder Niko lifted his other arm high and elbowed his double hard in the gut, but was met with a savage kick; he grunted and started sliding again, grasping at the beads of glass for purchase. Young Niko struggled to pull his gun arm out of the net but all his weight was on it now and the wire frame dug into his skin. Elder had grabbed his leg and was yanking on it; he kicked at the grasping hands, and as he did I remembered something vitally important.

"He's tied to me!" I screamed.

Elder laughed as Niko's eyes widened. "That's right, asshole," he shouted. "If I go, your boyfriend goes."

Niko bit his lip, recalculating, and pushed himself higher with a grunt, yanking his arm free. But as he did the gun caught on one of the glass baubles, and before he could grab it the weapon was sliding and scraping down the net. Toward the other Niko, who lunged for it, laughing.

In a clear mental flash I saw what would happen: he'd grab it, he'd shoot young Niko between the eyes; his face would go slack and he'd fall off the net into the void and vanish, and it wasn't that I loved him or couldn't survive without him but something else, a pure flash of righteous indignant anger rising up in me. After coming back for me, after *rescuing* me, when he could and maybe should have left me behind, he didn't deserve to die like this.

Elder was stretched out precariously, hand only inches from the gun, and without thinking or planning I grabbed the rope trailing up to him and yanked it, with all the strength I had.

He let out a *whoof* as his torso lurched back, all the air forced out of him, and balanced for a heartbeat at a crazy angle, only one foot touching the jangling net. Then momentum pulled him backward, over the side, and he fell.

Everything happened very fast.

The gun slipped through a gap in the net and tumbled into darkness.

Elder screamed in fury and grabbed for the edge of the net. He caught it and the whole thing twisted; but he'd snagged only a single strand and it couldn't stop him. It shrugged him off, slicing the skin off his fingers, and he fell, arms and legs flailing, trailing rope behind him.

But his grab for the net had dislodged my Niko too, and he was head down and slipping, flailing, grasping, tangled up in Elder's rope.

All this happened faster than movement. Maybe my brain had sent signals to my muscles, but they hadn't arrived yet, or my body was too confused to interpret them.

Elder tumbled down, rope twisting behind him. He reached toward the cylinder, but it was too far away; he was going to fall past it. He stretched for a piece of furniture instead and collided with it, face scraping against the top of a sideways bureau; a spurt of blood exploded from his cheek even as he scrabbled to get a grip but he was moving too fast, and he kept falling.

Above me, my Niko cursed and slid off the edge of the net. The tangled rope had gone taut and yanked him off, and he was falling too. Only he wasn't tied onto a rope. He wasn't tied to anything.

I finally moved, lurched forward to do something, anything. But Elder had fallen out of my sight line around the curve, and his end of the rope tied to the bed I stood on snapped taut with a creak, wrapping tight to the cylinder's curve.

Young Niko plunged by on the edge of my vision, colliding with a piece of furniture and tumbling with it. Before I could think, before I could stop myself, I threw myself off the edge of the cylinder after him, arcing down into nothingness.

≫ 15 ≪

I'd never skydived or bungee jumped before; I had no experience with free fall and barely any even with contact sports. My angle was wrong. I realized this as my foot left the wood of the cylinder, realized there was no way to correct my course. I'd shoved off at too steep an angle. I was going to fall beneath him.

Desperate, I reached my hand up, but he was one step ahead of me. He couldn't reach me, but grabbed for the rope trailing behind me, tied to my ankle. Then it went taut and I jerked to a stop, the rope around my leg yanking me back with a stab of pain and flipping me upside down. I swung in sickening arcs, head twisting from side to side trying to understand what was happening, but for a moment nothing made sense, my headlight strobing through images I couldn't assemble into a coherent whole: a length of blue and white rope, a swinging body, a line of dusty floorboards. Frantic, I reached up and grabbed the rope, pulling myself more or less upright, swaying dizzyingly.

I took a breath but it didn't help.

I dangled thirty feet below the cylinder, two ends of the same rope rising to curve up its top side towards the anchor of bed they were wrapped around, now out of sight. Beneath me, Elder Niko swung from his end of the rope. His side happened to have been longer and he'd therefore come to a rougher stop than me; he was gasping, momentum swinging him in sickening arcs over the void beneath us.

I looked up for younger Niko, and immediately regretted it.

He'd stopped his fall by grabbing hold of my rope, but he wasn't tied to it, and was far enough above me that the bottom side of the cylinder was within reach, upside-down furniture bolted to its surface. And before I could open my mouth to scream *No!* he leapt for it.

He arced across empty space, smashing into an overloaded and upside-down black bookshelf that I'm pretty sure was an IKEA Billy. He grabbed for a shelf but it pulled free, designed to resist only force pulling it down; books flew everywhere, but Niko's grip flashed to the solid side of the bookshelf and he jerked to a halt, clinging like a confused squirrel to the angled side of the bookcase.

The rope creaked uneasily. I looked down. Elder Niko was climbing his rope, hand over hand. Murder in his eyes.

I leapt up mine, for a second sure I'd be faster. I had a head start. I was twenty years younger.

But my life hadn't been given over to surviving down here, to stalking, to killing. And my slack coiled beneath me: a leash, tied to my waist.

Elder reached the loop and hung his full weight on it.

I slipped four feet before my grip on the rope was firm enough to stop me, friction-burned hands screaming.

Below me, he laughed, and sprang up the rope like it was a ladder. My arm muscles were already aching. Before I could pull myself up more than a foot or two, his hand closed around my ankle.

I strained to pull away, kicking. I looked up. Younger Niko's gaze met mine; he clung to the slanting bookcase, skiwampus, casting around for a way to help, but there was nothing in reach. He couldn't help me.

I looked down and saw the same face, shriveled in a blink by decades of rage into something monstrous.

"We don't have to do this," I panted, still trying to shake my leg free from his cold grasp. "We can all go through, get to the surface. Then go our separate ways. Like you said."

"You fucking idiot." With the hand not gripping me he fumbled at his belt. "You thought after all this time down here I'd *forgive* you? That we could be friends again like old times? No. You're going to die. And then I'll hunt that bitch down"—his eyes flashed up to his younger clone—"and kill him, again. First things first, though." And he reached up with the knife he'd unclipped from his belt, flipped it open, and sawed into my calf.

I screamed, trying to pull away, but his other hand gripped my leg tight, and I looked up through the pain and starred vision at my Niko's shocked, helpless, too-distant face, and below me his double laughed and kept sawing with terrible strength. In one fierce thrust he sawed through my jeans and into my skin, and drew the serrated blade back, cutting deeper, into flesh, into muscle.

"It's your fault," he grunted, and the strength drained from my hands as hot pain sliced through me. "I went looking for you. You know that? How I got lost." My blood dribbled onto his face and he spat it away. "We had a fight. Don't remember. What about." He pulled the blade back and I screamed, trying to twist away, but he only gripped me more firmly. "But I remember hating you. I remember that. I remember hating you and deciding to go back anyway. If I hadn't, if I'd turned around, I would have felt the sun again." His breath was ragged. He shifted his grip on the knife. "But I went back. For you." He sawed the blade deeper and I screamed and realized, then, that I couldn't escape this, couldn't escape him, that if I didn't die from falling or bleeding out or being left for dead the best I could hope for would be a life down here in the dark, like him, left to wander forever, trapped, helpless, lost. Fighting it was impossible. It was already done and settled, and had been from the moment we'd first set foot Downstairs, from the moment we saw the house, from the moment we'd first met.

"He won't forgive you, either." He grimaced up at his younger self through teeth stained red by my blood. "He just hasn't realized it yet."

"He's not you," I gasped, "he'll never be you." And because I couldn't make myself believe it I stomped down on his face as hard as I could.

He let out a *whoof* of air and something crunched as a splatter of blood arced out into darkness. His eyes rolled up into his head and he went limp, and then he fell. In thirty feet he reached the end of the rope around his waist and it jerked him to a horrible stop, flailing his limbs like a scarecrow. He dangled there, spread-eagled, face up, over the void. Unmoving.

Somewhere above me Niko was whooping in victory, but I barely heard him through the blood thumping in my ears, the high-pitched scream of pain in my leg. Refocusing my eyes, I dragged them down. The knife was still embedded in my calf. As if from a great distance, I reached with one hand, gripping the rope tight with the other, and pulled it free in a queasy sucking motion. Blood dribbled down my pant leg, dripping off my foot. Numbness and pain rippled through me, and muscles spasmed in my arm, but there was something I had to do before any other concerns. Woozy, I pressed the knife to the second rope, and started to saw.

"No, wait!" Niko shouted down at me. "The key! Do you have the key?"

I looked up, blade held against the rope. "What?"

"To get back to our side." His voice seemed distant, swallowed up by empty space. Maybe I was losing more blood than I realized. "The doorway's close. It has to be. But you need to get the key."

Front pocket, right side.

Below me, Elder Niko still swayed at the end of his rope, eyes closed. Motionless. I didn't think I could have killed him, but I must have knocked him out.

Or he wants you to think you did, anyway.

I still held the knife against the rope. Loose white innards strained free from the cut I'd started, escaping the tension of the deadweight below.

But the cut was still shallow, tentative.

Uncommitted.

I nudged the knife closed, shoved it into my belt.

"Hurry," Niko hissed above me.

"Thanks," I muttered. "Helpful."

I started down.

I climbed fast, muscles trembling. The silence unsettled, now that no one was talking or scrambling or trying to kill anyone. It felt like the surrounding darkness was a blanket, muffling, infinitely thick. A dangerous unreality was taking hold, like this was a video game. A dream. I shook my head, fighting mental fog. Tried to feel the pain in my leg, to let it be an anchor to keep me from floating away.

I got to the end of my rope and realized I had a problem. When I'd looped it around the bed I hadn't bothered to even out the two sides. And now, at the end of mine, I was still a few body lengths above Niko. I couldn't reach him. His side had happened to be the longer one, and the only way down to him now would be climbing the last few feet on the other end of the rope. His end.

Which meant detaching myself from mine.

With one hand I scrabbled pitifully at the knot, but untying it was hopeless for half-a-dozen reasons, my weight on it not the least. There was only one way to get off my rope onto his.

Below me, Elder Niko let out a gormless groan, head lolling to one side. But his eyes stayed closed.

A strange clarity had descended on me, the disconnected panic that comes from piling bad decisions on bad decisions, realizing you've gone too far but no longer able to stop. Shifting my grip to Niko's rope, I flipped open the knife again, and before indecision could paralyze me, I cut through my own rope, just above the knot at my waist.

It was done. His rope creaked as it took my weight. I tried not to hear it. Tucking the knife into my belt, I lowered myself the last few feet to Elder Niko's body.

He was still splayed out, spread-eagled, face up, eyes closed. Blood and spittle drooled from the corner of his mouth.

His fingers twitched in gentle spasms, the last motions of a dying insect.

We were surrounded by darkness. The faint streetlights miles below, the pools of desk lights and floor lamps above, bookended but did not penetrate the dark we swam together in.

Gripping the rope with one numbing fist, I reached out with my other hand, fingers brushing the edge of his pocket. He groaned again, flopped his head sideways.

I pushed my fingers inside, feeling for the key.

There.

I pulled it free, carefully, gripping tight as the tines tugged the lining of his pocket, caught on its edge. I focused all my attention on not dropping it, not letting it tumble down into oblivion; on pulling my hand slowly, deliberately, out of his pocket.

Which is why I didn't notice his eyes had opened. Not until his hand closed around my wrist.

"The fuck," he muttered, lids heavy, speech slurred, "you doing down there?"

His grip on me was weak, but I felt the gathering awareness in him, like a coiling viper. His face was smeared with blood, and more had rushed to his head as he dangled, making his face look misshapen, swollen. One of his pupils had dilated all the way open, and a blood vessel in the eye had burst, a spidery red blotch reaching tendrils through the white. He looked monstrous.

"I let you swim through first," he muttered, eyelids fluttering closed. "Can't remember. Why. Guess I thought I still owed you. A debt." He blinked, coughed. "Stupid. Wrong. Couldn't find my way. Back up. Think about that mistake every day, every day, every day..."

I let him rant. Delusional.

But I saw him then with a sudden chill clarity. I understood he was only monstrous because of what I'd done to him. And I'd only done it because of what he'd done to me.

We were our own vortex, circling, wanting to converge but never meeting in the middle. Dragging each other down, deeper and deeper and deeper.

"I'm sorry," I said, gently pulling free of his grip and slipping the key into my pocket. He scrabbled at my waist with his other hand, pathetic, as if trying to get a grip on my belt to pull himself up. "Sorry for dragging you down here. You deserved... someone better than me to be your friend. And you can hurt me, hunt me, kill me as many times as you want but it'll never change that. Never take it back." I took a deep breath. "But I can't let you do it any more. You don't deserve to die, but..." My eyes flicked up, then back to his. "Neither does he."

He smiled, blood spilling from the corner of his mouth, and as it dribbled away something changed. Like the light had shifted, popped a shadow into a shape. Like noticing the gorilla in the crowd.

The confusion in his eyes had been a lie. They were perfectly clear.

"Too bad," he said, "no one gets what they deserve."

He had the knife in his hand. My belt. He'd slipped it off my belt while I was babbling.

I swung sideways as he lunged it at my face, and it nicked my ear. There was no grogginess in him, no disorientation. I'd just seen what I'd wanted to see, one last time. I'd never really seen him at all.

My muscles tensed to fling myself back up the rope, but without the knife I'd never make it. Never be free of him. Certainty flushed through me. This had to end. This had to be the last time.

He lunged again and I grabbed his wrist, wrenching it backwards, trying to pull the knife free. He snarled and reached for me with his other hand but I twisted away. We swayed and twirled at the end of the rope, the rope I was no longer tied to, clinging instead with one desperate, trembling hand. I felt fibers snapping as the cut I'd started above us frayed, grew larger. One way or another this was about to end.

He stabbed at my face again and I swung to the side, just enough for his hand to brush past me, so I bit down on it as hard as I could. He swore as I ground down harder, feeling flesh give, tasting blood. Sensing his grip loosen, I snatched the knife, his expression of shock burned into my vision even as I turned away, already climbing. Maybe I'd never done that before, in all the times he'd attacked me. Maybe I'd never fought back.

I climbed, the knife clenched between my teeth. For a fleeting moment, and maybe for the first time in my life, I felt like a badass.

But I'd bought myself only seconds and not enough. I'd pushed well past the limit of my endurance. I barely had the strength to pull myself up. I'd put a few body lengths between us, but he could swallow that lead in seconds. I was a wounded rabbit limping from a wolf.

Below me something screamed and I realized it was him; a terrible scream, rage and pain and loneliness and betrayal etched onto air. He started up the rope after me.

"Get. Back. Here." He growled. "Get the fuck. Back down here. I'm not finished. With you."

Bloodstained rage twisted his face. He was gaining. He was going to kill me.

And then a dictionary clobbered him in the face.

I looked up, shocked, at a triumphant Niko shaking a fist down at us. "Leave him the fuck alone, dickweed!"

He'd clambered up on the tilted side of the bookshelf, another heavy hardback already in his hand. He hefted it, gaged the distance, and flung.

The angle was awkward for throwing, and this time the missile went wide, plummeting down into darkness with its pages aflutter, like they wanted to take wing. But he'd already grabbed another book.

Below me, his elder was shaking off the blow.

I climbed.

Niko kept throwing books, and some collided with my pursuer, enough to throw him off balance, to buy me more seconds. I needed every one. I was fading fast, and so was the rope. Muscles tore and fibers snapped. My vision shrunk to a wavering tunnel, only my hands and the rope visible in the deepening blackness. I climbed. I climbed with some reserve of strength I'd never guessed I had.

I reached the notch in the rope and climbed a few feet past it, spit the knife into my hand, and began to saw.

"Faster," someone was muttering, maybe me, "faster."

The Niko below flung himself up the rope. He'd almost reached me.

A crushing inevitability pressed into me, from tingling arms to kicking feet. Someone had already won. Someone would live. The clock would run out and we'd find out who.

Faster.

Fibers twisted, stretched, broke free.

A copy of *Dhalgren* arced smoothly by my head.

Guttural noises just beneath me. It was too late. He was here.

And then the rope split.

He was at my feet. He flung himself at them when he heard the tear of the rope giving way, but had nothing to push off, no momentum to save him. He scrambled frantic as the rope went weightless in his hands, a finger brushing my shoe.

Then he fell.

Within a second he'd plunged past the range of our lights, swallowed by blackness. Only then, after losing sight of him, did he scream, and there was no fear in it at all. Just rage.

But it was a tiny sound, lost in vanishing darkness, fading

fast and not repeated.

He was gone.

PART THREE

MANIFOLDWISE

Some things do through our judgment pass
As through a multiplying glass.
And sometimes, if the object be too far,
We take a falling meteor for a star.

"Ode: Of Wit," Abraham Cowley (1618-1667)

≫ 16 ≪

I woke up from a dreamless sleep to face the unpleasant truth that we couldn't stay here forever.

Getting back on top of the cylinder had been like navigating an especially surreal and challenging climbing gym. From his perch on the bookshelf, Niko had scoped out a route from one piece of furniture to the next, and then, in what would have been the most viral parkour video ever if YouTube had been invented yet, leapt from one to the other, till gasping, he scrabbled up to the top of the tube. From there he could pull me up; all I had to do with my shredded muscles was keep hanging on, although that was hard enough. Once we'd made it, I thought nothing in the world had ever felt so good as lying on my back on a floor, every muscle gloriously unclenched.

Wedged in between two dressers, so as not to roll off the edge, we slept.

When we woke we ate power bars from Niko's pack: my own had gotten lost somewhere in the fight, probably sliding off the curve and down into the darkness below. I had no idea where to go from here—although it seemed like there were only two options, one way down the tube or the other—but Niko had found a better option while he'd been scrambling around up top. Directly under the invisible anchor point of the densest part of the web, the chandelier itself, was a trapdoor. It opened downward with a creak when you pushed on it, releasing fold-up stairs like the ones that sometimes climb into attics. The stairs descended some fifteen feet to a cement floor bisecting the cylinder. Its upper half was a domed tunnel, vanishing into the distance in either direction. Bare bulbs hung from the roof every fifty feet or so, leaking dim puddles of yellow-orange glow. Water ran down the center in a foot-deep trench, fast enough to gurgle.

We kept to the level ground on either side of the trench, and started trudging.

We moved slowly. Niko had cleaned up the cut in my lower leg as best he could, bandaging it with some socks from a dresser drawer and a tight-wrapped bungee cord from his pack. But it hurt, a lot. I hobbled more than walked, had to stop for frequent breaks, or lean on him for support. He helped me without comment, when I needed it.

I couldn't help notice, up close to him like that, that he seemed to have all his fingers.

Unsaid things festered between us.

The tunnel had no perceptible slope, but the water in the trench ran fast, rushing eagerly past us. The path curved gently left, then gently right. We walked for what felt like a long time.

Gradually, the perfect curve of the ceiling began to straighten. The roof above flattened, the curves at its edge sharpening, until they squared off entirely. At the same time the tunnel gradually shrunk back to house-sized dimensions. Presently we were walking down a rectangular hall of concrete, like some forgotten subbasement in a shuttered factory. It felt like we were back "inside" again. The sensation of walking through a pipe suspended over empty space receded, and we felt once again embedded in earth.

There were no side doors, no other stairs up. There were no decisions to make. We just walked. Other than an occasional grunt or word of coordination, we didn't speak. A small part of me wanted to ask a million questions. Another part didn't want the answers. There was a tautness between us, a strain, like a handshake stripped down to bone and gristle, rubbing, raw. It had been there a long time, underneath everything we'd wrapped around it.

Mostly we were just too tired for talking.

Up ahead, the tunnel ended in a cramped room. After a few more minutes of trudging we reached it.

It was a squat and vaulted brick antechamber, maybe twelve feet across and hexagonal, with tunnels coming in from all six sides. Each seemed identical to the one we'd entered from. Water flooded the sunken floor of the chamber and ran out the trenches in the middle of each tunnel.

In the center of the room, under the water, was a stubby concrete pillar topped by a metal hatchway with a wheel, like something you'd see on a submarine.

I knew before checking that the hatch would have a keyhole.

Once we confirmed it did, we became strangely hesitant, our momentum lost. We perched on the lip of a tunnel, dangling our feet in the water, using the excuse that we needed a rest.

There was so much I should be asking him, so much I should be saying, but I couldn't find a way to start.

Well. I had pretended nothing was wrong for such a long time. Maybe another few minutes wouldn't hurt.

The rippling sounds of the water were peaceful, and I didn't want to break the silence. But someone had to.

"So." The sound bounced off vaulted brick, making the chamber even more claustrophobic. I coughed. "We've come all this way. We going through, or what?"

He seemed curiously reluctant, but managed a weak smile. "Sure! Yeah. Let's do it."

We waded over to the hatchway. The wheel was inches under the surface of the water. I pulled the key from my pocket and slipped it into the lock, and it went in smoothly. I spun it through a full turn till it made a tiny *chunk*, then turned the wheel. After a few revolutions, something gave, and we found we could swing the circular hatch open along one hinged side.

We held our glowsticks underwater near the opening. The hatch opened into an ordinary-looking but flooded room beneath us with a yellow-tiled floor. Chrome and porcelain rippled up at us. We realized after a moment it was a flooded bathroom.

"If this portal thing leads through a toilet," Niko said, "I'm out."

We could only assume the way through was somewhere out of sight, around a corner or down an unseen hall. But how far?

"The other guys are probably doing the same thing on their side," I said hopefully. "Maybe we'll swim through at exactly the same time, go past each other."

"Huh." I looked over; he was staring uneasily into the flooded opening. He caught me looking and forced a smile. "Why not, right? Makes as much sense as anything else." But his gaze slipped off me and up to the vaulted ceiling, like he was interested in the architecture. He wasn't.

He was worried about something.

I turned away, ignoring the upwelling of unease, and frowned at the hatch. There was something familiar inside it. I squinted, trying to make the wavering underwater shapes resolve. Tied to something just under the hatchway was a climbing rope, the same kind we'd used with our Grip Monkeys. It stretched down in a taut line out of sight, towards the hidden wall of the room beneath us.

Niko'd seen it too and reached into the hatch to give it a tug; it seemed taut. "Thirty-five meter rope," he said. "Looks like someone marked the way through."

"Our doubles?"

He shrugged. "Sure."

"And this goes through to another hatch like this one, you think? One that opens up onto our original side?"

He nodded, still not looking at me. "What my evil twin was

looking for. The way back through. And if we're lucky, our doubles will be waiting on the other side. Just like this. Getting ready to swap places, swim through. Get everyone back where they belong, all neat and tidy."

"And, uh. You know this how?" I swallowed. Here was the discussion I'd been too afraid to start, happening anyway.

He tensed, frowning at his submerged shoes. "I don't *know* it. But we might as well believe it, because if they're not there, and there's no more synchronicity between us at all any more? Then who the fuck knows where this rope leads." He shook his head. "No. They're over there. We have to believe that. They're having this same discussion, right now."

"*They.*"

My voice broke and he looked up startled, guilty, afraid. Like a texting jaywalker realizing too late he's wandered into traffic.

"Niko," I said, trembling. "Are you sure you're... I mean, when we got separated..."

Somewhere far below us, something *groaned*, low, immense. The ground quivered, like a mountain turning over in its sleep, and the surface of the water pinched and jittered in sympathy. We both dropped half into a crouch, but the earthquake stopped, the low rumbles far beneath us faded. The water we stood in sloshed drunkenly.

"What the shit was that?" I breathed.

"I don't know." He nodded, coming to a decision. "But we'd better hurry this up. So. You should go first."

"Excuse me?" I blinked.

"You're the better swimmer." He was talking fast, shooting uneasy glances at the walls around us. "If there's anything un-expected or it's too far or whatever, you can come on back. But if you make it through safe, tug the rope a couple times and I'll follow."

"I thought we'd go together." Something was wrong again. The dark circle of the submerged porthole was ominous. Unknown. This was happening way too fast. "I don't want to go alone."

"It's the only way." He gazed at me, fierce. "Orion, just trust me, okay? This will all work out, but you need to trust me right now. Can you do that?"

I wanted to laugh. *Trust?* Could we *trust* each other? The question unraveled into a million strands, tendrils stretching back through everything that had happened down here, and everything that had happened before that.

"No." I shook my head, mind racing. It felt like riding a bike that kept slipping gears, nothing quite fitting together, accelerating down a hill with less and less control, no way to stop. "No. I can't do this again. Why won't any of you be honest with me? Stop it. I know. *I know.*"

The ground trembled again, and Niko took a staggering step toward me, grabbing my arm. "Stop," he gasped, "Ryan, stop. Don't say it."

"He showed me a finger," I whispered.

"Shut up," he shouted. "Look. Here's what's going to happen. You and your double will swim through together, then me and mine after, and everything will be *fine.*"

"But the other Niko," I gasped, shaking my head, "he's—"

The ground dropped out from under us, like a plane hitting turbulence. Rumbles quivered in stone far below. I tripped and plunged into water up to my neck as the earth swayed, groaned like a buried titan coming back to life.

Niko grabbed my arm and pulled me up, put his other on my shoulder, pulled me against him and shouted in my face: "Shut up! Shut up, you fucking idiot, stop talking, stop overthinking everything and just swim through the goddamned tunnel, just swim the fuck through, it's the only way you're going to—" And he cut himself off, biting his lip, his eyes filling up with tears.

And then I got it.

Synchronicity.

I felt like we were balanced on an impossibly heavy pivot, a mountain peak turned upside down. If we leaned too far in any direction...

Two soap bubbles, pressed together, floating in a vast empty void. Trembling.

He knew. He knew there was no other Niko to swim through. Not any more.

The surface of the water twitched, rippled. Waiting.

He let go of me, took a step back, face reddening. "I just think," he said quietly, miserable, "that you should go first, okay?"

The walls around us crunched, coughed, like millions of brick bones having chiropractic work done.

Maybe it was my imagination, but the room seemed smaller.

And then something else hit me. Something so hard and huge I forgot how to breathe, and staggered back away from it.

I let you swim through first. Can't remember. Why.

Bricks cracked and popped around us, exploding like popcorn.

Couldn't find my way. Back up.

He was reaching for me but I tripped backwards, reflecting his concern with horror. *No. No, no, no.* As each brick popped others surged into the gaps they made. The walls were squeezing closer. The room was barely nine feet across, now. Water surged into the runnels leading out, cascading away in all directions like it, too, was terrified.

"It's okay," Niko was saying, smiling through the tears. But it wasn't. He hadn't been close enough to hear what his elder had been whispering. *He didn't know.* "If it doesn't work I'll just stay on this side, retrace our route. No biggie. Get back to the top and so what if there's some headaches. I'll deal."

"No." I shook my head. "This can't be what happens, it's not right, it's not fair, it can't end like this..." Something was slipping from my grasp. I tried to hold on to all the stories I'd told myself about Niko, about me; all the endings I'd wanted for us. Each of them were tales disguised as truths; worlds that I yearned to slip into like tailored gloves, sized just right; stories reassuring me that I finally understood what I deserved, good or bad, where I belonged and who I belonged to, and who belonged to me, where I didn't have to be afraid that I'd love the wrong person or the wrong person would love me.

But people don't wrap up like that into nice little cages, contained. We weren't each others' stories. I wasn't Bradley's and Niko wasn't mine and I wasn't his, no matter how much at times we'd wanted to be. We'd mistaken shadows for substance, all of us: chased them and failed, of course, to grab them, become shadows ourselves in failing.

But we weren't shadows. We were more than that. We deserved more.

Something swayed inside me, as if I'd let go of one handhold and gripped another, shifting my weight even though I wasn't sure the new grip would hold. But by then I'd already done it, already committed. And it held. It didn't let me fall.

"No," I said again, but stronger this time, stepping forward into the shrinking space, barely the size of a closet now and still getting smaller, "No. This isn't how this ends."

And as the words bounced off the contracting brick that had nearly reached our heads, it held still. The rumbles and groans around us went dead. Everything paused. Everything held its breath.

I looked at him and I tried to see him. Really see him. I willed the layers of muck and confusion between us to pull back, to clear away and reveal someone, at last, who I could understand. The Niko who forgave me. The Niko I'd hurt. The Nikos I'd saved, damned, slept with; the ones who needed me, who hated me, who wanted me dead. The one I'd tried so hard to find, looked everywhere for, down here, up there, inside us both and beyond possibility.

None of them were here. The only one here was him.

"You don't owe me anything," I said, "but I owe you this. At least this." My voice was hoarse at first but I willed more of my growing conviction into it. "Maybe you're right and going through together, coming face to face with it, would be bad. But maybe not. You think it's coincidence that every cockeyed theory we've had about this place has turned out right? I don't. If it's feeding off us, multiplying us, then we're the prime factor. The base case. You think that if we see the truth, we'll be destroyed. Well, fuck that. I reject it. I reject it with every ounce of my goddamn being."

I took a deep breath. "Maybe synchronicity matters, maybe it doesn't. I don't really give a shit. What I want is to get us both back home. Look, I don't deserve your trust, and maybe I don't know how to give it to anyone else. But if I have to start somewhere I should start with myself. And I think I can do this. I *trust* I can. Okay? I made Tiger Shark in swim club and I can hold my breath for three minutes and I can make it. I can make it through. I can. And you are fucking coming with me, because I may be the reason you're down here but I swear to god I will also be the reason you get back out."

The words lingered in the air. We stayed suspended for a moment, unable to break eye contact, afraid, maybe, to look at anything but each other.

A single brick tumbled from the ceiling and made a tremendous splash. We both started, then laughed, and couldn't stop laughing. We were buried alive and almost certainly going to die but goddamn, we were going to do it together.

"Yeah." He took a breath, then another. "Yeah, okay. We'll try it your way. You win. This time, dipshit."

It was decided. It felt good, and yet painful, too, as some pinprick of knowledge stabbed into me, saying even if we did survive, nothing would ever be the same between us. So without overthinking it I stepped forward and hugged him, fierce as the roiling lump in my throat.

His bare skin, still damp, felt hot against my own. He held me tight, wet curls rubbing against my face. Heat passed between us, but it was the least of what had.

We'd loved each other, at times. Even if the people we'd loved were mostly in our heads.

It was nice, but his curls were tickling my nose, and I pulled back before I meant to, reflecting his surprise at this with embarrassment. For a second it looked like he thought I was going to kiss him, and then I thought maybe he was thinking of kissing me, out of some kind of misplaced solidarity, and we both stood uncertain for a second or two before dropping arms and stepping back.

Awkward. But sort of perfect for the mismatched shape of us, which was, if nothing else, our own.

I turned away, toward the submerged portal, the way out, the way home. I stared down at it.

The thought of swimming into that hole without knowing the way to the other side stabbed a different part of me, the one concerned with oxygen and continued existence. I pushed the fear down but it kept manufacturing images for me: jeans snagging on hidden nails that held me back while I flailed uselessly; huge dead fish swimming the flooded halls with flaking gray skin, bulging eyes growing larger and larger as they closed on me. I imagined drowning. Breathing water instead of air. Spasms of lungs. Knowing you were about to die, only not soon enough. Not nearly soon enough.

Almost on autopilot I guided Niko through what to expect, through breathing exercises, stroke technique. Calming him down as much as myself. Preparing.

We started to breathe, deeper and deeper. Priming our lungs with all the air we could.

I stared at the circular opening, visualized the motions I'd make. I tried to believe I could do this. I tried to push down the sliver of doubt lodged somewhere in my throat.

Gripping the sides of the hatch, I paused. I wasn't ready. But if I waited any longer, I'd never be.

"Last one back to the right dimension buys the drinks," I said, then took one last huge breath and dove headfirst into the hatch.

The flooded bathroom was lined with tile that might have been a pale yellow but glowed red in the light of our glowsticks. Chromium sink fixtures and a frosted-glass shower threw back fiery light. In contrast to the other flooded chambers there was no mold, no algae, no water damage. It might have been flooded seconds before.

I didn't pause to wonder about this, but kicked off through the open door into a murky hall, following the guide rope which led onwards like Niko had predicted. He followed behind, pulling himself hand over hand along the rope.

I focused on my strokes, old swimming lessons coming back. This was a different sort of lane, of course: the floor brown carpet, plaster-of-paris above instead of a shimmering boundary of air. And the wounded leg slowed me down: it hurt, every time I kicked. But I wasn't worried, not yet. I had good lungs. I could swim for a while.

The rope turned a corner into a large unfurnished room with a half-dozen washers and dryers piled in a corner. We swam past them, mechanical, calm, following the rope through an open doorway opposite.

Through the door was what looked like a small porch or mud room. Boots and shoes tumbled weightless in the water. The rope stopped here, tied to a capped metal pipe. The opposite wall was a sliding glass patio door.

The airlock.

Through the glass it was dark. But faintly, through water rippling as if moving with strange, hot currents, there: another sliding door. Distance was impossible to judge, but it couldn't have been more than twenty-five or thirty feet away, suspended in a dark and empty void.

And framed in that window was a figure, silhouetted by the red glowstick he was holding.

Another me.

It could have been a mirror, except he was alone.

The water trembled and around us foundations groaned, but I reached down and grabbed Niko's hand and held it tight against the wriggling water, and he gripped it back. We stared across the gap at my double, defiant. I realized half the sick anxiety I'd been feeling was from my growing proximity to him, subsumed by the general terror of what we were doing. But that wasn't why I gripped Niko's hand so tight.

We were breaking the rules of this place. Staring asynchrony in the face. And we weren't backing down.

We were going through anyway.

The rumbling petered out, died away. Shoes disturbed by the shaking drifted around us, their long laces waving like antennae.

All this had taken only seconds. I knew every one mattered. Across the gap I saw the other Ryan reach for his sliding glass door, and found myself doing the same, unsure which of us had moved first.

In lockstep, our doors slid open, and we swam forward into the black water between, me tugging Niko behind. As we reached the portal the floor and ceiling dropped away. Everything was dark.

And as we swam past the threshold something *changed*.

The water cooled; the pressure and ambient sound in my ears shifted. The other sliding door was just ahead of us, but it seemed too as if we floated in a cavernous space, a space beyond measuring, the other door impossibly distant. Disoriented, I turned around to shut the one we'd come through—remembering they couldn't both be open at once—and as I did another shock of *change* swept through me, crystallizing into something immense, yawning, terrorful. I remembered the spring Elder Niko had spoken of

this stream

deep at the roots of this place: a spring that split and split and split again, endless. I felt possibilities branching in the water around me, but even more in the waters inside me, in the part of me inside the waters. Branching, expanding, growing like mold in a petri dish but spilling out of the dish now, spreading through the lab into the walls, the world

A looking-glass held

and it was as if I was the mold, the spring, an effervescent source spilling out into infinite variation, branches branching and branched again into an unfillable space, filling it. Boundless, multiplied. Multiplicious.

Slowed by dream-syrup, fighting awed stupor from these whispers of immensity, I turned my back on that powerful water at the center, pulled the glass door shut, staring numb as it slid implacable down its track, while behind me the other Ryan did the same. Our doors clicked shut.

And as we turned around to swim across that heady gap, facing each other again, we both raised our glowsticks high. And then we saw them.

Drifting in that immense and empty space, lit a gangrenous red by our chemical lights, there were more of us.

Dozens. Floating, unbreathing. Eyes open.

Watching.

I screamed, bubbles of precious oxygen exploding from my mouth, and then they came for us.

I twisted around and yanked the handle of the door, but it wouldn't budge. I clawed at it, slammed my fist against the glass.

The door wouldn't open and they were right behind they were coming they were going to get us and

I twisted

wildly, pressed hands to the glass behind me, but it was hopeless. There were too many of them, drifting forward with hands outstretched, serene expressions on their faces. Beside me, Niko was preparing to push off against the glass and make a break for the other side, but faltered as he saw what was happening across from us.

The other Ryan had failed to open his door, too, but as he'd turned around a coincidence had pried apart our synchronicity even further. There were more of the floating Ryan-things on his side—an accident of distribution maybe—and the few seconds Niko and I had to act had already run out for him. As he bent his legs to push off from the glass door, they reached him.

He screamed, eyes going wide as their fingers wrapped around his hair, caressed his arms, reached pale white fingers into his mouth. Bubbles of air exploded from it as he twisted frantically, trying to shake them off. Hands closed around his neck, twisted his arms, pulled his head back by his hair to a terrible angle; hands that seemed unsure if they meant to caress or kill. He was panicking, writhing in the water like a trapped eel, dying.

Before we could move or even start swimming forward to help him, his body spasmed as he breathed in.

He *breathed in.*

It's a horrible thing to watch yourself drown. My brain disconnected, floated away, observed only in abstractions as the me across the gap spasmed and convulsed, surrounded by things that shared our face, pressing forward, closer, eager, like they wanted to feed off the flicker of his death. The guttering red of his thrashing glowstick was doubled, reflecting mirrored patterns in the glass behind him.

Something was wrong with that.

More of the Ryan-things were drifting toward us, Niko was

yanking frantic at my arm, but I couldn't move, couldn't react, struggling to grasp that fleeting thought like a half-remembered dream. Neurons tried to spark. The doubled reflection. Something had almost slipped into place.

A glowstick and its reflection, now gone horribly still. But the closer one was occluded by the swarming forms, the shadows that swam around it.

The one in the reflection was clear. In the glass, its light was unobstructed.

In the glass, there were no swarming figures. They weren't real.

They weren't real.

There was no way, no time to explain this to Niko. So I wrapped my arms around him tight, felt for the glass door with my legs, shut my eyes, and pushed off hard towards the swarm of encroaching Orions, as hard as I could.

The pain in my wounded calf went white-hot but I barely noticed it. I shot straight forward, intent, right through the mass of things closing in.

Something brushed my leg. I kicked forward with all the strength I had. Two fingertips bounced off my forehead, trailed through my hair, but we were moving too fast for them, we were through, we were past them. I'd done it.

We'd reached the glass door on the other side; below us, the drowned Orion sank into erasing darkness, no longer struggling. I couldn't help him. But Niko was kicking and thrashing in what I'd assumed was terror at the illusory Semblances. To pull the door open I'd have to let him go. But as I did I realized the reason for his panic was far more serious.

He was out of air.

Whether he'd lost the last of it screaming, whether his smoker's lungs were just inferior to mine: it didn't matter. I could tell at a glance he wouldn't make it to the other side. He wouldn't even make it through the door. His face was filled up with crushing desperation, a look that counted seconds until the overwhelming urge to breathe took hold of him. They were almost gone. His lungs were empty.

So I pressed my mouth to his and filled them up. I gave him the last of my breath.

His eyes went wide as he realized what I did, and I could feel him fight to pull back, to stop me. But I held him tight, and anyway I knew he couldn't stop the desperate need of his lungs to expand, to survive, no matter what his forebrain thought it wanted.

In moments, it was done. I was empty, and he was full.

He would live. He would be the one who made it.

I pulled back, and as I did the water exploded around us like it had come to life, gone in a snap from still to carbonated. All around us the architecture groaned, flexed, heaved, like it too had come alive.

Across the gap of thrumming water behind us I saw the glass door we'd come through pull back. Its dimensions and the reflection of my glowstick grew smaller.

The wall was pulling away.

Desperate, my own need to breathe becoming overwhelming, I faced forward again and tugged the glass door beside us open; but even as I did, Downstairs expanded. Plaster dust pillowed into the flooded hall in thick weightless clouds as the walls split and reformed, split and reformed, like bones breaking and healing and rebreaking, growing fractionally longer each time. New glass doors spawned above us, below us, to every side. I ignored it all. I pulled the door open along its rail and grabbed Niko's arm to shove him through.

He gripped the edge as I did, twisting around to grasp my shoulder. There were no words for the look on his face, or for all the things we'd never said to each other and now never would. There was no time to say them and no air to say them with. I could guess what some of them would have been, maybe, but not others. There was so much of him I'd never really seen, never understood, too caught up in manufacturing other versions of him in my head to know the only one who'd really been there. Now I'd never know how much I'd missed.

I pulled back gently from his grasping hand, and smiled, and tried to put everything left I wanted to say into that.

Water frothed around us, twisting, expanding. And then in a flash it began to move. A current tore him from me, limbs flailing, pulling him backward through the mudroom and down the twin of the hall we'd swum through to get here, toward the other hatch. I hoped. Toward the right surface. Even if I'd wanted to follow, I couldn't have: another current of shockingly cold water had wrapped itself around me like a tendril. An angry, biotic undertow pulled me down, straight down, with vicious force. The reflection of my glowstick strobed as the current pulled me past door after door of sliding glass, faster and faster: a flicker, then a dull throb, fading and mingling with the phantom patterns and flashes of color now dancing across my vision as my oxygen-starved brain began to shut down.

In a moment I'd breathe in, and I wondered what it would be like to inhale those waters of possibility, let that multiplying spring inside me. Let it fill me up. I harbored no illusions, of course: I'd seen it happen to the other Ryan. I'd die. But a beautiful way to go, in the abstract at least. A life spent worrying about possibilities would end by drowning in them. Neat.

This peaceful thought had so taken me I was caught utterly by surprise when the current shifted and smashed me into a pane of glass with so much force it shattered. Rocketing through a waterlogged hall of turbulent water, surrounded by tumbling fragments of glass, head throbbing and vision expiring, I opened my mouth in shock and, before I could remember I was waiting for a poetic moment to die, breathed in.

But love that moulds one man up out of two,
Makes me forget and injure you.
I took you for myself sure when I thought
That you in anything were to be taught.

"Ode: Of Wit," Abraham Cowley (1618-1667)

I hope this finds you well, if it finds you at all.

I walked by our old house this morning. The whole yard was flooded, caution tape everywhere. Empty driveway. Whoever lives there now must have abandoned ship while they waited for the plumbers to sort it all out. But it gave me an idea.

Water gushing up from the basement windows. A mess. But I found a little whirlpool in the swamp of the front yard, a big exposed pipe sucking liquid back in. Back down. That's where I'll drop this, I suppose. That pipe might just lead to the city sewer system, but if I'm lucky, it goes a lot deeper.

Maybe it would be better to let you keep thinking I'm dead. Maybe I shouldn't be writing this. But I think you'd rather know. There's a difference between dead and gone, despite the expression. I think you'd prefer knowing one Ryan, at least, survived. I never really did understand how you think, but I'm reasonably sure about that.

Assuming, that is, you survived too.

I think you did. That could be me projecting, one last time. But I don't know. It feels right that one of each of us made it out. Balanced.

Not synchronous, but resolved.

I don't have headaches here, which is weird, because it's not the place we started from. Elder Niko said there weren't just two sides, and I thought I got what he meant, but I've stopped trying to pretend we ever understood Downstairs. Anyway, it's different here. Chewing gum isn't a thing, and this asshole named Ted Cruz is president now, which feels like the worst possible timeline, but still. No headaches. This universe is not rejecting me. Maybe I should be insulted, but I suppose I'll have to take what I can get.

You're not here. I'm pretty sure of that. Hopefully you ended up back where we started. Hopefully that part of the plan worked out.

We never understood Downstairs, but that hasn't stopped me making up new theories. And I think we were wrong, about a lot of things.

Well. Duh.

But for example: we always assumed our doubles were on the other side of the fridge from us. But I don't think that's right. I think it was worse than that.

Sure, they were trapped just like we were when the fridge connection was broken. But we were wrong when we thought they'd been looking for a way to get back through. Because they were back already, where they belonged, on their own side. The problem was that two doppelgangers had followed them through.

Us.

They figured it out a lot quicker than we did, I think. How that loss of synchronicity had pulled our twin houses partially apart, like a gardener starting to separate two potted flowers. How the easy way back had been sheared off.

So they had to figure out a different way to get rid of us. We were sleeping in their beds. Eating their food. Stealing their lives while they lurked below, afraid to come near us and push things even farther out of sync. Sneaking up to steal food in the middle of the night, thieves in their own house. And the only way to send us back was to find another connection point, a deeper one, down where roots still twined together. And prod us into finding it, too. They had a lot more time to explore than we did. Downstairs became their home.

They couldn't explain things to us, not directly. Because if we'd also realized how much things had diverged, it would have tugged our universes even further apart. So they tried to find the subtlest ways to send a message. Saying things without changing hardly anything. Tweaking the note, the video. Pulling us back from the dead-end of the furniture maze. Nudging us away from the red herrings closer to the surface, to deeper explorations. Toward the new way through they'd discovered. A flooded tunnel, buried deep. A way to get us back home.

I think about that a lot. We were their monsters. But they helped us anyway. Maybe they didn't see any other choice, but still. That was pretty great of them.

Once they'd found the flooded connection, they could pass through to our home universe, and help clear the way back for us. Leave guide ropes. Make it easy. One of them stayed to keep an eye on us, to make sure we "discovered" the flooded tunnel. Once we did, the plan was probably that they'd swim back through in advance, so that, when the time came, all four of us could pass each other, and the two of us could keep holding onto the thread of belief that synchronicity wasn't broken. At least until we were all in the right place again and what we believed no longer mattered.

But then that other Niko crept up from the depths of possibility and fucked everything up. They didn't see that coming, I don't think. How could they have?

Bitterness, multiplied. Multiplicious.

Your counterpart, the other Niko from the twin universe—he didn't make it. *I always kill the Nikos first.* Well. That's what happened. I saw a finger, and I think, I'm guessing, you found a body. I can't even imagine what that must have been like. But that's why you thought the plan was fucked, that synchronicity was going to collapse the moment we survivors confronted the fact that only one Niko was left. Elder Niko's plan was to take his place, but without him, there was a gap. A flaw in the pairing. And based on everything we knew, you were sure it was a fatal one. It almost was.

Who knows how much of this the other Ryan figured out. I guess all he knew is that his Niko never came back. He must have been scared, confused. Maybe that's why more of the Semblances went for him. Maybe it wasn't coincidence.

So that's my theory. Probably wrong. I'm sure you have your own.

I guess the details matter less than how we left things.

It feels like too late and too little to say I'm sorry, but I am. I was lost back then, too afraid to grow up and too wounded to risk being wounded again. But that's not a good enough excuse. I should have been more honest with myself. I should have been more honest with you. I wasn't, and I hurt you, and I can never pay you back for that.

I am enclosing ten bucks, though, for the drink you bought me that night at the Russian dance club, lest you think I'm a total mooch. I did say I'd get you back, didn't I?

Thinking back on it all, I do take some comfort that when push came to shove, we choose to save each other rather than turn our backs. Or maybe it wasn't a choice: that wasn't how it felt to me. We just did it. You saved me, on the bedroom tube above that awful void, and other times besides, when you had every reason to leave me behind. And I gave you the last of my air, not because I didn't want to lose you, but because you were the one who deserved it. That other Niko said it's too bad we don't get what we deserve. But deserving's just another story we tell ourselves, you know? And sometimes, if we try real hard, we can tell it right.

I should wrap this up. If I spend all day writing mysterious letters to another man, my boyfriend might get jealous.

Devin. That's his name. Devin.

Maybe it's ridiculous to think something as tiny as a triple-bagged USB key wrapped in a ten-spot could possibly find its way to you. If our two universes connect at all any more, it's far down in knotted skeins, hopelessly tangled. I imagine this baggie winding its way through miles of piping, tumbling down moss-covered tunnels, floating through submerged, warped bedrooms. Somehow making its way back up to another surface, another flood. Seems silly. But I see it in my head, vivid. I try to believe there's a world where it could reach you, even though the odds seem astronomical.

On the other hand, with so many possibilities down there, maybe it's inevitable.

Irrational, but true.

I haven't dreamt about you in years, but I did last night. Not in particulars. Your name just sort of floated through me, troubling in some way but not defined. A word repeated until it loses its meaning, becomes obsessed with itself. A reflection's reflection. It's why I came by the old house, but all that was here was a flooded yard. All it reflected was me.

I never knew what we were to each other back then. Something less than all those things we never were, but more than a friendship. An else-ship, maybe. An other-ship. Traces of mingled shrapnel under shared skin. Broken pieces of each other we tried to make our own.

I guess we're left with what we had. *Have.* Definitely have, yeah? Because we're gone to each other, but not dead. We survived.

So hey. I hope you're doing all right and you found your way back to a world where people say "fourd" like God intended. I hope you found better people to hang out with and a new set of hobbies and someone to appreciate your fashion sense. I hope you realized you were someone worth saving, too.

I miss you sometimes, but that's okay.

We made it. And I think we'll be alright.

Nah. Scratch that.

I trust we will.

Get Your Own Unique Copy

Subcutanean is a permutational novel: the text can be rendered in millions of different ways. This was a fixed copy generated for sale on traditional platforms, but your purchase entitles you to your own free digital copy with a unique seed number that will never be re-used. Your unique copy will contain a slightly different version of the story: words, sentences, even entire scenes may appear there that don't appear in this version.

To get your unique copy, send an email to: **aareed + subq @ gmail.com** with this passphrase: *the wolf is real.* You'll receive your version as a Kindle-compatible .mobi file, unless you request a different format: PDF, .epub, Markdown, or plain text versions are also available.

You can also find out how to get a paperback copy with a unique seed by visiting the project's website at **subcutanean.tex-tories.com**.

ALTERNATE SCENE

Here's a scene from Subcutanean in a different rendering from the one in the main text of this version of the book.

(From Chapter 6...) "I did some digging on your address," she said, "and found something rather interesting." She turned the last two words into an annoying sing-song. *Raaaaather intressting.* Trying to tune her out, I opened the file and pulled out the first page.

It was a blurry copy of an old newspaper article, maybe from around the turn of the century. I didn't see the relevance until a few contextual clues started popping out at me ("by the new university"; "on top of the hill") and I realized where the entrance to this cave was. I almost choked on my tea.

It was about a search for two kids who had gotten lost in an underground cave, dating from a summer in 1931. Two neighborhood boys, 15 and 17, had gone exploring in the caves and never come back out. Rescuers sent down had heard faint voices, and it was suspected the pair had been boxed in by rising water. Brave men had tried swimming through flooded passages, but none had been successful at reaching the boys. Some rescuers had proposed digging a shaft down to them from the surface, but none could agree where to dig: different rescuers had heard the voices coming from very different places, saying very different things.

The next article, dated a day later, was a short history of the cave, most likely a filler piece given a lack of new rescue details to report. The cave had been a source of trouble before, it seemed: a forbidden but popular spot for local youths, it had never been mapped but was not believed to be extensive. But it was treacherous in part because of a spring which bubbled up from its depths with unpredictable rhythms, sometimes flooding lower passages or resmoothing upper ones. The spring's varying flow erased markers and made it hard to tell the twisting tunnels apart, making the cave seem "far larger than its true extent." It had no official name but the locals had given it various nicknames, among the most popular of which was Looking-Glass Cave, after the clear pool the spring waters sometimes left at its entrance. The article explained that this was a reference to a Robert Louis Stevenson poem taught in local schools which all the kids knew, and which the article reprinted in its entirety. Some of the verses seemed uncomfortably on-the-nose.

> *Sailing blossoms, silver fishes,*
> *Pave pools as clear as air—*
> *How a child wishes*
> *To live down there!*
>
> *We can see our coloured faces*
> *Floating on the shaken pool*
> *Down in cool places,*
> *Dim and very cool*

I flipped to the other few pages in the folder as the woman twittered on about her sleuthing skills in the county archives. The remaining articles painted a grim picture of the subsequent week of rescue attempts, the breathless updates unable to disguise the fact that all had failed. Squabbling about the proper dig site, fears of digging too aggressively and causing a cave-in, a surge of flooding from the spring which was flowing "with unusual vigor" that season, and ever-growing crowds of spectators all delayed and complicated the rescue efforts.

The final article was short, the tone terse, only the headline betraying a hint of pathos: CAVE SEARCH CALLED OFF: SURELY NO HOPE LEFT FOR YOUNG SPELUNKERS. It announced that after fifteen days the rescue efforts had been abandoned. No voices had been heard from anywhere in days, and the boys were presumed drowned, starved, or buried—dead, one way or another. The cave entrance was to be sealed for good, the spring bricked up to prevent its no-longer-pure water from reaching the surface. No future generations of children would stare wistfully into its pools clear as air.

With the article, for the first time, were pictures of the two boys.

They stared out from oval windows, sketched in ink, probably sourced from the descriptions of grieving mothers rather than life. They looked younger than their reported ages. I stared back at them, unable to stop from wondering what their story had been, what it must have been like to die down there. Alone except for each other. Had they been lifelong friends? Or casual schoolmates exploring the cave on a whim? Did their final days bring them closer together, or tear them apart?

ABOUT THIS COPY

There are several hundred places in the master copy of Subcutanean *where text can vary. Here is a sampling of some of the decisions made by the rendering code when this copy was generated.*

- Your narrator was a bit more optimistic than the norm.
- Some proper nouns in this copy that might be different in others include Semblances, Grip Monkeys, and *Dhalgren*.
- Your versions of Ryan and Niko found the ladder to nowhere.
- Your Ryan and Niko found the spiral hall.
- Your Niko didn't fall when climbing the vertical hall.
- Your copy of *Subcutanean* contains this stats page.
- Your version of Ryan spoke to Bradley on the pay phone.
- In this version, the final fight took place on a tube of bedroom-stuff suspended over an endless dropoff.
- In your ending, Orion swam through the final gateway with Niko, not alone.
- Your epigraph authors included Walt Whitman and Abraham Cowley.

ABOUT THE AUTHOR

Aaron A. Reed is a writer and game designer focused on exploring new ways for authors and readers to tell stories together. His award-winning games have been featured at IndieCade, South by Southwest, Slamdance, GaymerX, and the Independent Games Festival, and he has spoken about digital storytelling at Google, PAX and PAX East, WorldCon, NarraScope, and the Game Developer Conference. He holds a PhD in Computer Science and a MFA in Digital Arts and New Media, and aims to continue abusing them both in interesting ways.

This is, by some definitions, his first novel. Or maybe that was *Blue Lacuna*. Or *Hollywood Visionary*. Or *The Ice-Bound Concordance*. It's hard to say.

Aaron lives with his totally real boyfriend in Santa Cruz, California, in a house without a basement.

Reviews wanted! Please share your reaction to *Subcutanean* on Goodreads or anywhere else readers congregate. Your voice is a huge part of helping an indie book like this succeed. **Thank you!**

AARONAREED.NET

Printed in Great Britain
by Amazon

29091933R00130